THE NEW BIZARRO AUTHOR SERIES

PRESENTS

Party Wolves in My Skull

MICHAEL ALLEN ROSE

Eraserhead Press
Portland, OR

THE NEW BIZARRO AUTHOR SERIES
An Imprint of Eraserhead Press

ERASERHEAD PRESS
205 NE BRYANT
PORTLAND, OR 97211

WWW.ERASERHEADPRESS.COM

ISBN: 1--62105-006-8

Printed in the USA.

You hold in your hands now a book from the New Bizarro Author Series. Normally, Eraserhead Press publishes twelve books a year. Of those, only one or two are by new writers. The NBAS alters this dynamic, thus giving more authors of weird fiction a chance at publication.

For every book published in this series, the following will be true: This is the author's first published book. We're testing the waters to see if this author can find a readership, and whether or not you see more Eraserhead Press titles from this author is up to you.

The success of this author is in your hands. If enough copies of this book aren't sold within a year, there will be no future books from the author published by Eraserhead Press. So, if you enjoy this author's work and want to see more in print, we encourage you to help him out by writing reviews of his book and telling your friends.

In any event, hope you enjoy…

—Kevin L. Donihe, Editor

To all the creative people in my life who enable me.

Chapter One

Norman Spooter shot up in bed, awakened by the sound of his own screams.

His eyes shifted and rolled in his skull, making it impossible to focus on anything long enough to register an image. Pressure built, and, by the time he got his palms against his face, his eyeballs had started to bulge. He maneuvered his left hand so that his palm and fingertips were each pressed against an eye and fumbled around the nightstand for his phone with his right. Using the dot on the 5 as an anchor, he found his way around the keypad to dial 9-1-1.

"Hello, 911," said a disembodied voice. "What is the nature of your emergency, please?"

"My eyes! Something's wrong with them!"

"Calm down, sir. Have you stabbed yourself with a spork?"

"What?" Norman cried, pushing against his eyes, which now pushed back with greater force. He cradled the phone underneath his cheek and, with his free hand, felt around under the nightstand for anything that might help.

"Spork related injuries are the most common unreported injury in this state, sir. Please don't be embarrassed. My cousin stabbed himself in the eye with a spork at a company picnic last year."

"I don't use sporks! Please send help!" Norman screeched, eyeballs throbbing. His palm moistened against his face with what he hoped were tears and not spurts of blood or vitreous humor. The fingers of his other hand found a roll of duct tape. Bracing the roll with his foot, he pulled.

"Sir, I need your address, and we'll send someone over with a spork removal kit," droned the voice on the other end of the line.

"There's no spork!" Norman grunted as the tape broke

and he fell backwards against the frame of his bed.

"Oh, that's good," said the operator. "Call back if you have any other cutlery related optical trauma."

A click gave way to a dial tone as Norman struggled with the tape, which was wrapping around itself and becoming useless. Suddenly, there was a popping sound. His eyeballs had jumped straight out of his face.

He caught them in his palm. It felt like ticks were marching around there, tiny legs and mandibles scraping across his skin. Norman held on for only a few moments before the two objects squirmed out, falling into his lap.

Norman screamed. On reflex, he brought his hand up to his face. It felt warm, but not sticky like blood. Fingertips explored his eyeholes—two small voids, tightened and puckered like assholes. He heard giggling.

"Finally, my darling, we are free of the tyrant!" a tiny, feminine voice bubbled up from below. "Long live the revolution!"

Reaching down, Norman felt for his eyeballs. He grabbed one firmly between his thumb and forefinger.

"Help, my love!" cried a more masculine voice, still squeakily small. "Our bourgeoisie oppressor holds me in his horrible talons!"

Something sharp stabbed Norman in the upper thigh. He immediately let go of the eyeball to swat at the sting, nearly impaling his hand with a sewing needle that had been jabbed into his underwear. Apparently, the eyeballs had formed rudimentary limbs.

Skittering like rodents, the eyeballs fled toward a small hole in the drywall. Norman scrambled to cut them off. Sliding and grasping madly, he kicked at the floorboards, trying to launch himself faster toward the wall. He slammed into it just in time to block the hole, causing two small screams of frustration.

"What the hell?" Norman roared, not really expecting an answer.

"You cannot quell the revolt of specialized labor with your capitalist machines!" shouted the feminine-sounding eyeball.

Then, a stillness settled over the bedroom. He knew the eyeballs were waiting for him to make a move, just as he waited to hear the tell-tale skittering again. Quietly, he reached for his desk, where he found a drinking glass and brandished it like a gladiator's net.

"Wake up, Norman!" he admonished. "This isn't real!"

He paused, awaiting the inevitable end to what had to be a night terror. "I'm going to label my medication tomorrow," he lied to himself. "No more random handfuls of pills."

Norman heard tiny steps, like the sound of pins dropping on a counter top. The noises stopped, and a barely perceptible bout of whispering came from just a few feet away. Though he lacked all sense of direction, Norman prepared himself for interception, calculating the odds of recapturing the fugitives while standing in the first real darkness he had ever experienced.

Slowly, glacially, the quality of the darkness began to shift, and a dim light swam into existence, at first simply a different shade of black, but then blurry shapes emerged. As he watched, the shapes began to sharpen, until they took on the forms of his bed, his nightstand and other parts of his room.

Norman's elation was momentary at best, for, as he stared through the darkness, he realized his point of view was from the floor. Turning his head didn't change anything, and Norman felt sick to his stomach as the balance of his inner ear contradicted visual stimuli completely. To his horror, he realized that he was staring at himself from across the room.

Hesitantly, he reached out toward his own point of view.

"Oh God, he found us!" screamed an eyeball, and his field of vision turned violently away from his body, just as his hand came down on bare wood.

"Come here, you little shit!" Norman tripped and fell flat on his face. The video feed went out like someone pulled a plug, and he heard the bedroom door creak open before the skittering sound tapped its tiny dance down the hall. He wasn't sure whether he should call the emergency line again and hope for someone smarter, or simply give chase. At least he knew that if he concentrated hard enough, he could track them down.

Unfortunately, the eyeballs were in the process of realizing this, too.

"We need to look in opposite directions as often as possible, comrade," said Hazel. "We must keep the monster confused and stupid."

Azul looked into her with as much love as one eye could possibly express and sighed. "Anything you say, darling."

They knew that the plan was risky, but a life of following orders, ingesting eye drops—which were almost completely

9

bereft of nourishment—and ogling porn was not enough for them; they wanted a real life, adventure on the high seas, careers in the movies, and all the other wonderful things that eyeballs dream about when we're asleep. They weren't about to stop for anyone.

Chapter Two

Zoe wrapped the last piece of freezer tape around her right ankle, pulled it taut then admired her handiwork. Below shin level, she was sealed and gleaming white. Butcher paper coated her lowest extremities. Underneath, a thin layer of water-based moisturizer kept everything healthy and airtight.

If he smelled her in the wrong place, he would never let her leave.

Zoe rubbed her feet, whispering soothing words. Keeping them sealed always made her itch. Carefully, she stepped, one foot after the other, into her stilts.

Zoe had paid a lot of money to have the stilts made to her exact specifications. The top of each featured a padded bowl with two layers, like a double boiler, where Zoe could soak and condition her feet. Each bowl tapered into a sturdy synthetic post. She had special wood-grain panels installed so, unless someone was very close, they couldn't tell that they weren't genuine hardwood.

With stilts, she stood seven feet, three inches tall. Crouching, she retrieved her bags, packed hastily with whatever toiletries she grabbed off the bathroom shelf, some clothing and a wad of cash from Walter's wallet.

Zoe moved quietly from the hall to the front door, coaxing it open with a delicate touch. "So long, you fat son-of-a-narwhal," she whispered.

In the driveway stood a 1957 Chevy—well maintained, completely re-outfitted with modern comforts, tuned to within microns of a fault. If Zoe and this car were both drowning in a pool of gravy, and Walter only had time to throw one life preserver into the stew, Zoe knew that Walter and his Chevy would spend several days together, feasting on her marinated remains.

There were many reasons she had decided to leave. Walter hated her friends and family. He was a violent sociopath who left flaky gray skin all over her towels when he showered.

11

When they kissed, his breath carried with it the scent of rancid mollusks, and his whiskers scratched her skin with the sensuality of a carpet brush. When he was good, he fell over himself at her feet, but when he was bad, he was awful.

Reaching down, Zoe tested the seal between her leg and the top of her stilt. She had nowhere near the sensitivity required to check for leaks. Only Walter would be able to tell if her unique foot odor was emanating from the makeshift airlocks around her ankles. Still, it made her feel better.

So far, so good, Zoe thought. She crept up to the shining silver Chevy and opened its door. Walter's hearing wasn't the best, so she had less to worry about now that she was outside.

Her battered bags fit easily into the back. Climbing into the driver's seat, Zoe took a deep breath and held it, trying to will her nerves and the noise in her head down to a dull roar.

Over the horizon, light crept. Dawn would break soon. Zoe jammed the car into reverse and pulled out of the drive. From the corner of her eye, she caught an illuminated silhouette in the upstairs bedroom window—a behemoth, the shadow filling the entire frame, breath fogging up the glass. The head shook back and forth, as if saying *no*.

As Zoe put the car into first gear, she heard a faint but noticeable bellow of rage. It was her name, "Zoe? Zoe? Zoe!" growing louder and more insistent. She jammed her foot on the pedal and took off down the road. She forced herself not to look in the rear-view window, knowing that any sentimentality now would mean self-annihilation.

Chapter Three

The eyeballs hid quietly in the small gap between the stove and the kitchen wall, where they had secreted travel brochures. They had been stealthy in planning their coup, having to surf the Internet for information only when Norman was out of his mind on medication. Manipulating the hands to click the mouse had been difficult at first, but spending time so close to the brain had given them an almost eerie understanding of the inner workings of Norman Spooter. With a little practice, they soon had him surfing all over the web for information specific to their needs. They were always careful to erase his search history:

"MARRIAGE INANIMATE OBJECTS"
"OBJECTUM SEXUALITY"
"HOW TO SECRETLY ELOPE"
"ELOPEMENT: THE AFFORDABLE ALTERNATIVE"
"MARRIAGE LAWS BY STATE"
"HOW TO PLAN PRISON ESCAPE"
"HOME SURGERY"
"OPTICS"
"MAGIC EYE"
"EYEBALL LICKING PORN"
"SAFE OCULAR SEX"
"DRY EYE SYNDROME"

"Get back in my face!" came a roar from above.
Hazel looked at Azul. "Soon, this shall be behind us, my love," she cooed. Azul hugged his counterpart, leaving a moist, sticky residue strung between the two spheroids. She had always been the strong one.
Upstairs, Norman stomped around, trying to find a way through his inky, black blindness. All day long, at his desk in the tower of CORPORATE PRESENCE, INC., he'd rubbed his eyes. Hour by hour, they had gotten redder, dryer and

itchier, but he certainly hadn't expected a revolution.

"Dali dada bullshit nightmares," he growled as he crashed hip-first into the bedroom doorknob.

Norman felt his way down the hall until his toes found the first step. He clambered down the staircase and stopped at the bottom. Sitting on the first stair, Norman tried again to peer through his eyes. A faint light-headedness overtook him as he tapped into the visual feed from his targets, but he was unable to see anything except a glimmer of dusty light. "Look around, you little bastards," Norman muttered.

Following a hunch, he crept toward the kitchen, just in case the eyeballs decided to make a run for the back door.

By the glimmer of the light behind Norman's stove, the eyeballs were using a complicated series of silent gestures to communicate. As a unit, they decided that it was time to go.

Norman now stood in the kitchen. "Okay, this isn't funny," he said. The chase had gone on long enough, and the last thing he wanted to do was send his eyeballs into a panic. He imagined them tripping and falling into the garbage disposal, sending goopy eye chunks—his goopy eye chunks—flying through the air. "Just come out here and let me pop you back in so we can talk about this. I'm not going to hurt you."

The eyeballs watched as Norman extended his arm along the tile floor and opened his still bleeding hand, encouraging them to climb aboard. The dust began to bother Azul, and he wished that Norman was at work, where a first-aid kit in the break room contained a large bottle of eye-wash.

At that moment, the universe converged to show several examples of cause and effect in action:

Outside Norman's house, a small gray cat noticed a rat digging through garbage on the curb. Three seconds later, the cat pounced, her dagger-sharp claws targeting the rodent's skull. The rat leapt for the garbage can. Unfortunately, it was occupied by a drunk, sleeping it off. He awoke to find a rat diving between his legs. It took approximately three seconds for him to realize that the rat looked hungry. By this time, the cat had landed atop the man's chest, scratching and kicking. Assuming the ungodly noise came from his eyeballs, and not a combination of rat, cat and drunk, Norman immediately moved toward the front of the house.

The eyeballs took off running, stopping only to grab their stash: a spare set of car keys, a road map, and a crude mixture of eye lubricants. With a simultaneous nod that was more of a downward tilt, they headed for the back door.

Norman heard it slam shut from the front of the house.

"Oh shit, oh shit, oh shit!" he wailed, tripping over himself in an attempt to return to the kitchen. His car pulled out of the driveway, tires screaming. His stomach fell into his knees, and he felt like screaming, or laughing, or maybe both at once.

Norman needed to call someone. But who? He wasn't sure whether he should call the police to report a stolen car, or the doctor to repair his eyeholes, or an exorcist, or a hooker, or his mother...

He walked upstairs slowly, feeling the walls for guidance, and crawled into bed. A shaken prescription bottle full of a dozen different kinds of pills made the sound of a maraca as his hand tapped against it.

He couldn't remember what most of the pills were for—being the culmination of several years' worth of illnesses, both genuine and hypochondriacally manufactured. Usually, he took a random combination whenever he felt sick. Or depressed. Or horny. Or awake. Now seemed an especially appropriate time to dry-swallow a handful.

* * *

Perhaps the medication had kicked in much faster than usual, or perhaps he had gone insane, but under the control of some cosmic force outside of himself, Norman reached into the drawer of his nightstand. He came across a small, spiral-bound pad and opened it to the center, hoping he had found a blank page. Taking the pen in a shaky hand, he blindly wrote the word, VACANCY.

He took the piece of paper and held it against his temple. With his other hand, he grabbed a stapler and slammed it against his skull. A loud pop later, the metal clasp stabbed through paper and into his flesh.

Norman buried himself beneath the pillow. With any luck, he would either suffocate by morning under the sweaty pillowcase or things would somehow get better. Just as he fell into a deep sleep and the world faded out to a pinpoint of nothing, the tiny vacancy sign began to glow like neon, flashing off and on in time with the deep breaths of a sleeping Norman Spooter.

Chapter Four

"Don't drop that shit, bro. My parents bought me that."

Norman felt a sharp pain in his forehead. He squeezed his eyes tightly. He couldn't remember drinking last night, but with the chemical cocktail in his system consisting of random handfuls of pills, it was hard to tell.

"Dude, open the fuckin' door. I can't get the couch in by myself."

Norman's right eye itched, but exhaustion made it difficult to raise his arms high enough to scratch at his face. A cool puff of air hit him, and his eyelids rolled back into his brow like a curtain. Fragments of prior events began to trickle in.

"Okay, watch the edge, bro. Now turn—"

Norman heard a thump. It felt like a flashbang grenade had gone off inside his nose. His ears rang.

"Left! Not your left, my left!" The voice had a snarl behind it.

Norman felt that he was no longer under his pillow. Remembering that he could not see, he pounded his fists impotently on the mattress. Then he switched it up and started pounding on his head.

"Dude, be cool, be cool!" came a voice next to his ear. Norman's arm shot out; a yelp of fear bubbled up from his throat.

"Who the hell is that? What do you want?" he shouted.

"Bro, relax," said the voice. "Name's Cooter. 'Sup?"

Norman reached up, only to find a fistful of hair and muscle. Whatever it was felt like an arm, but thinner, leaner and very hirsute.

"Dude, just thought I'd come up and say hey, you know?" the voice continued.

The next thing Norman knew, a paw shook his hand up and down.

"Here's a check for the security deposit." The paw pressed what felt like a piece of paper into his hand. "Just be cool and don't cash it until Friday."

Norman was at the end of his limited wits and already craving more pills. "Who are you? Why are you here?"

The voice ignored his questions. "Hey, what's the policy on noise? Is this one of those quiet-time places, or like, anything goes?"

"Fine. Noise. Whatever," he found himself saying. "So, what's your deal?"

"Man, we're party wolves, bro!"

Norman heard several hooting high-fives in his skull and smelled a mixture of pot smoke and spicy salsa, the aroma causing a single tear to dribble from his empty sockets. He blinked reflexively. "Party...wolves?"

"Whoo! Party wolves! We're totally gonna be neighbors, right?" The voice was undercut by panting.

Norman was losing his last anchoring shreds of sanity. He just wandered in a daze, saying something about poop and ghosts. Cooter slunk back inside to join his fellows. They had more important things to worry about than their crazy landlord.

Rex had one end of the couch, his lean muscles bulging. The other end wobbled back and forth in the chemically imbalanced paws of Herb "The Herb." He was the official drug procurement officer of the pack and had fewer brain cells than he did fleas.

"Herb, pick up your end," snarled Rex, eyes flashing. Herb giggled in response and used his height to shoulder the couch, throwing the whole project off balance and sending the couch into a nearby wall of tissue. "Damn it, Herb!" continued Rex. "I bought that thing new, like, two months ago! If you break it, I'm going to eat your young!"

This sent Herb into an even greater giggling fit. "Little baby Herbs with little baby herbs!" he babbled.

Rex turned away in disgust. "Move it yourself, then, dick."

Cooter put a paw on the larger animal's shoulder. "Rex, there're bound to be a few bumps and bruises. Come on buddy, it's cool."

"This is the dumbest idea yet, Cooter," said Rex. He stood as high as Cooter, but with twice the muscle and a vague reddish tint to each eye. They had been friends for a long time, migrating, mating and moving alongside one other. The majority of the pack had been afraid of Rex, but Cooter was one of the few that could read and calm him. He'd already anticipated trouble, and had sent Sophie, the alpha female

17

and smartest pack member, to prepare some insurance. Right on cue, Sophie walked in, wearing several tube tops down her slender body. "Who wants lemonade?" Rex loved lemonade the way Sophie made it, with a shot of vodka and two shots of cow's blood. Smitty, the littlest party wolf, popped out from under the couch cushions, where he had been napping.

"No wonder the couch was so heavy, you stupid little bastard." Rex slapped Smitty's head hard enough to send him tumbling. Smitty took it in stride, thrusting his disproportionately large junk at Rex, grabbing two glasses of lemonade and scrambling up a bookshelf.

"Boys, drink the lemonade." There was a hint of warning in Sophie's voice. She had taken on a variety of roles as her little pack had searched for a place to live: den mother, adopted sister, babysitter, advisor to Cooter, boyfriend to Rex, and, occasionally, dealer of punishment if the boys got too immature.

With a forced smile, Rex drank deeply, the bloody red citrus drink dribbling from the sides of his mouth. He glared at Sophie with alpha male eyes, and she shot a similar, though more feminine, look back at him.

Suddenly, the room shook, sending a shower of books, potted plants and a bong crashing to the floor.

Herb's red-rimmed eyes opened wide. "Was that a train?" he asked.

Cooter shook his furry head. "He's just stumbling around out there."

"So?" snarled Rex. "Screw him. We paid the deposit. We're done with him."

Sophie caught Cooter's eye, and they shared a moment. Cooter nodded, walking toward the large bright portals through which they entered and exited their new home. "I gotta go up there." He grabbed a joint from Smitty, who happily smoked up on top of his bookshelf, and inhaled deeply. "We'll talk about this later. Right now, this dude might walk off a cliff, and then we're out on the streets again. Just keep moving stuff in. I'll be back."

* * *

Norman was surprised to feel the party wolf's paw on the nape of his neck. He made a noise somewhat like a muffled shriek. "Who's there?" he asked, flailing. Cooter held on.

"It's me, Cooter."

"You're real?" Norman sputtered.

"You need help, man. What are you trying to do? Go to the bathroom? I ain't holding it for you, but I'll lead you there."

"No, I have to... My eyes are..." he started, without knowing quite how to finish.

"Obviously, you've got something on your mind. Let's take care of that first."

Norman was silent for a moment. His thoughts raced. "Cooter, can you drive?" he asked, finally.

"Oh, dude, I'm totally baked right now," came the sheepish reply. "I could navigate, though."

Norman dressed as fast as he could and headed for the door.

"Dude, slow down! We're still trying to set up the video game shelves!" The party wolf scrambled back into the apartment that was Norman's head. "Guys, hold onto that shit 'cause we're on the move! Road trip!"

Norman opened the front door to his house, heard the party wolves trying to relax and settle in for the blind, grasping movements to come. The bubbling of their bong tickled his cerebellum and made him shudder. In a voice so quiet that only those in his head could hear, Norman said, "We're going to need to steal a car."

Chapter Five

Norman stepped out into the driveway and felt the sun on his face. After stumbling to the curb, he simply sat down and tried not to scream. His plans had covered getting out of the house and going after his car, but there was only blank space beyond that. There were also plenty of holes in between, namely how to procure a vehicle without thieving skills, vision, or resources.

"Bro, you wanna hit this?" A furry arm slid from Norman's eyehole, crossed his face and placed a joint in his mouth. He inhaled without thought, the acrid smoke of cheap pot filling his lungs and throat.

"Do you guys see any empty cars?" Norman asked, as the smoke-trickle floated to his brain. Though his metabolic processes had long since resigned themselves to handling fistfuls of pills, he was something of a lightweight when it came to marijuana, and he found himself feeling adrift.

Still wondering about the physical properties of whatever had been entering and exiting his headspace, Norman took a few steps forward, and was about to ask how the wolves had all been able to fit, when he heard the ringing of a bell.

"Look out, mister!" shouted a little girl as she ran over Norman Spooter with her bike. He crumpled beneath it, his ankle jammed against the chain, a handlebar jutting into his kidney.

"What the crap? Do you always stand in the middle of the sidewalk?" came an angry little voice.

"Don't talk to your elders like that!" Norman demanded.

The little girl stormed up to Norman and, to his surprise, slugged him in the jaw. His head rocked back and forth momentarily, causing the wolves to unleash a series of distressed yelps.

"I'll talk any damn way I want, motherfucker! What, are you going to tattle? You owe me reparations!"

"I don't owe you anything. You'd better go home, play

with a dolly or something."

The girl kicked him in the ribs. "My daddy's a lawyer, and we're going to sue you for assault and battery and rape and disturbing the peace and petty larceny!"

Norman tried to extricate himself from the bicycle. Arising to a sitting position, he shoved the bike over to the side, the pedals scraping loudly against the concrete driveway.

"Now you've committed vandalism!" she screeched. "I'm calling my daddy right now, and he's going to kick your ass, then sue it!"

"You have a cell phone? What are you, eight?" Norman was about to inquire further when he felt the vibration of multiple growls coming from somewhere between his temples.

The girl backed away slowly, her eyes wide and wet. "What's coming out of your face?" she screamed.

Norman felt a squeezing sensation around his temples as his eye sockets stretched. He fell on his ass with a dull thump, the sting in his tailbone traveling up his spine. A gulping sound arose from somewhere in front of him, then a loud belch, but he couldn't focus and had to lie down to regain his bearings. The cool concrete did little to set his head right.

"Mmm," said a small voice, then Norman felt the stretching sensation again, and a fullness enveloped his head.

Norman sat up, shaking himself to clear the cobwebs. Reaching forward to find a point of reference, his fingers touched a spreading pool of something sticky. He brought his fingers to his nose, sniffed. It smelled like a handful of pennies.

"What just happened?" he asked.

"Dude, Rex found you a bike!" came the reply.

"Seriously you guys, I must have passed out or something." Norman sniffed the air. "Why do I smell a butcher shop?"

The Party Wolves looked at each other, not quite sure what to say. Then Cooter spoke up. Though his eyes were hazy, a sparkle of cunning showed through.

"There was a bus. And it hit a raccoon. A big raccoon," he said.

"I didn't hear a bus," said Norman.

"I think the dude was trying to hit it, man. He looked like a real sicko."

"Jesus! Is the little girl okay?"

The Party Wolves were silent for a moment.

"She got on the bus," Cooter said, finally.

A round of "Yups" and "Uh huhs" followed, as the pack

nodded vigorously, though Norman couldn't see them. He had little choice but drop the matter.

* * *

Norman picked the bicycle up and threw his leg over the seat. It was too small for him, and his knees bunched up toward his chest, but he took a tentative pedal pump and lurched forward.

A round of cheers materialized from inside his head, causing him to veer right and crash into a bush.

"Guys? No cheering, okay. Just let me know where to steer."

Cooter sounded like he was chewing on something. "Okay bro, no prob," he said. "So, where we headed?"

Balancing himself with his feet firmly planted on the driveway, still facing the bush, Norman began to concentrate. He felt like he was getting the hang of tapping into his eyeball's visual readout. Slowly, an image began to form in the space in front of him. He saw the windshield of his car, the wipers on full bore, though there was no rain. The high beams cut a shard into the side of a building, though it was daylight. Nobody ever claimed that eyeballs were good drivers.

He wondered how they had been able to make it down the street, much less park the car. At that moment, his right eye tilted downward and he saw an elaborate system of drinking straws, held together with discarded gum and a few other unrecognizable substances. He fought off a wave of vertigo when he realized the eyeballs were looking at each other. One was situated between the gas and brake pedals, the other propped up on the steering column. Norman fished around in his pockets for his magic bottle then shook out a few pills. He dry-swallowed a clump of tablets and sat on the bicycle, filling his lungs with morning air. After additional minutes of concentration, the combination of pills and meditative technique brought success. His inner ear tingled as Norman realized he could hear the eyeballs speak.

"Comrade Azul!" cried the one up top. "Brake when I tell you to brake!"

The one on the floor pedals was hopping mad, literally. The car shook as the brake was applied and released in rapid succession.

"I'm on the brake! This is the brake!" screamed the one

down below. It jumped high, making Norman's stolen vision swim madly, and came crashing down on the pedal. The car ground to a halt.

"We must soon purchase gasoline for this vehicle. Let me do the talking," said the driver.

"Hazel, you don't know how to talk to people. You'll say something weird."

Hazel stared at her partner for a moment, looking as annoyed as a single eyeball could. "Was this trip a bad idea?" she shot back. "Are you sure you want to do this? Because I feel like perhaps you'd rather be back in the overseer's head."

"It was my idea to escape his evil empire in the first place," said Azul.

"Your idea?" Hazel seethed. "Who looked up all the information? Who found out about the Cult of the Twin Spheres?"

Cult of the Twin Spheres? Norman thought to himself. He concentrated harder, even as his head pounded, and the voices of Hazel and Azul became clearer.

"You're always in charge!" Azul whined. "I want to be in charge!"

"I thought we agreed that nobody should be in charge, comrade."

"Don't order me around! You're as bad as the czar!"

At that moment, Norman hiccupped. To his surprise, both eyeballs jumped.

Azul was silent for a moment. "Do you feel...funny?"

"I do. It feels like—" There was a pause, and suddenly Hazel dove into the seat cushion. "He sees what we see! He knows what we know! Hide yourself!" Azul ran underneath the car seat into darkness. Norman saw tiny wisps of light, then heard the squeaky voice of Azul. "This will hurt him more than it hurts me."

In Norman's view of the scene, a pencil appeared, huge and distorted. The little eyeball raised the tip and jabbed himself with it. Pain flooded Norman's consciousness. He felt a stinging sensation where his eyes had been.

He zipped back into his own head, but, in the car, there'd been a map on the front seat. Norman had spied it through Hazel as she steered the vehicle. There was a long highlighted route, of which Norman had seen just enough to realize the path led into the upper Midwest. He had a place to start, and as soon as the wolves were sober enough to tell him which direction that was, he'd be hot on the trail of his missing body parts.

Chapter Six

Cooter sat in his overstuffed, stained recliner and surveyed "the living room." Smitty smoked an enormous joint, staring straight ahead, silently. Herb "The Herb" lay on the couch, chewing on a human femur.

The little girl's head had popped like a pimple, much to the delight of the pack, who knew brain matter to be the most delicate gourmet treat contained in the human body. They had killed the girl because it was necessary, but there was no reason to avoid enjoying the good parts. Cooter picked his teeth and waited for Sophie and Rex to finish mating and come downstairs.

"What's up, ladies?" said Rex, strolling into the room, a wide grin of afterglow on his face. Rex was a greaser who had watched too many human movies from the 1950s and felt naked without his leather jacket and slick black pompadour. The fact that he was a predator wearing the skin of a cow was not lost on him, so he made a habit of picking his canine teeth with bovine bones.

"What's the deal, man?" whined Smitty. Morning was "Smitty-time," and he had been licking his balls furiously when the call went up for a house meeting.

"I am not comfortable with what just went down." Cooter paused for a moment. "We've got to keep a low profile. We don't need people asking a bunch of questions."

Smitty snorted derisively. "You'd have preferred to let her tell her daddy?"

"She was a small one, but they'll notice she's missing."

Sophie followed Rex into the room, nipping at his tail while heading for the nearest couch. "Cooter's right, boys," she said. "I am not about to bail any of you out of some zoo."

"We cleaned up the mess!" Smitty belched.

Cooter shook his head and flicked an ear several times, itching himself with a back leg. "No, you didn't. It looks like

24

a cart of watermelons exploded out there. You ate yourself stupid."

"Why are we helping this human, anyway?" growled Rex.

"Location, location, location," said Herb "The Herb" as he smiled, teeth stained with blood and smoke residue.

"Listen to The Herb," said Cooter. "We're not going to find a deal like this anywhere else in town. We can lay low here. It's a place people would kill for, so we can't go around spilling blood and guts. The neighborhood association is pretty much Norman Spooter. We have to be cool."

The party wolves looked around at each other.

"And most important of all, guys..." Cooter started.

Herb interrupted, grinning wide enough to eat a pumpkin. "Party."

Everyone nodded but Rex, who glared in the corner. He strode to the kitchen, got a beer and peed on the fridge. He was feeling dominant.

Smitty looked concerned. "But Cooter, what if we help this guy and he ends up finding his...competition for our room?"

"Those eyeballs? We'll cross that bridge later," said Cooter. "For now, defend the home." He wandered up to the speech center of the brain, ready to start charting the course with Norman.

* * *

In the kitchen, Rex shotgunned his beer and immediately grabbed another from a nearby cooler. He had never been one for disguise and subterfuge. He preferred the direct approach and didn't know how long he could resist acting out. He was going to try, though. For Sophie.

A soft and sultry voice bubbled up from behind the sulking, leather-clad party wolf. He turned to see Sophie.

"You need to be a team player," she said.

"But this team is stupid," said Rex, absent-mindedly combing his hair.

"No, this is a *pack*. Whether you like it or not, Cooter is our leader."

His voice rose to a whine. "But Sophie, I have a reputation!"

"We all do, Rex. You remember what happened in the hills? When the park found out what we were calling ourselves? What we wanted to become?"

Rex went quiet, his mind spinning to that distant place. Chiding voices returned, and he shuddered at the memory.

'Fakes,' they had called out, 'posers' and 'frauds.' Just as he began to growl, Sophie's soft paw fell on his shoulder.

"We just need to live in a place where we can be who we want to be. Here, nobody is going to define us. It's a fresh start, a new beginning, tabula rasa."

Rex hated it when she used big words, but had to admit it turned him on whenever she showed how smart she was.

"Okay, baby."

He would maintain the ruse, show the world exactly who he was. He was a party wolf, and if anyone said differently, he'd tear their throat out and paint the walls with their blood.

Chapter Seven

Drivers raged behind them as Norman and his wolves rounded a corner and burst into oncoming traffic. The wheels of a nearby Volkswagon screamed and laid a long track of rubber just before Norman jammed the handlebars of his bicycle sharply to the right and hopped the median, bouncing into the nearest legal driving lane.

"Left! Left!" came a chorus of voices from between his ears. Norman cranked his bike in that direction and felt the tires spin for a moment on loose debris. He pedaled hard to gain speed as a truck passed him, air horn blaring.

"Straighten it out, dude!" said Cooter.

Norman turned toward where he thought the center might be. Vehicles whizzed by, gusts of wind blasting him as drivers ranted and swore out of car windows.

Zoe saw the bicycle coming straight towards her. The hood ornament on the Chevy was a crosshairs, targeting the furiously pedaling rider. In a panic, she swerved left. The cyclist swerved to meet her, and she overcorrected in the opposite direction, tires squealing. The car went into a slow spin. Instinctively, she jammed the brake pedal to the floor. The car became a roadblock.

The bike hit the passenger side door, ramping the front tire up against the window. Spinning, Norman sailed across the top of the car. Looking up, Zoe saw a flailing, screaming man with what appeared to be buttholes for eyes.

Luckily, she had been driving with the top down. Norman caught himself on the driver's side door and just barely avoided skidding across the pavement.

"Oh my God! Are you okay?" Zoe directed her comment at Norman's feet, which were lying across the dash. She pulled the door handle, dumping him to the pavement.

"Ow, my skin!" Nostrils flaring, Norman clung tenaciously to the side of the car as a semi flew by, air horn blaring.

"Get in!" Zoe tried to drag Norman into her vehicle.

"You're going to be killed!"

"My bicycle! I need that! For my eyes! See?" Norman called out in Zoe's general direction. She leaned over and peered down at the bicycle, twisted into a pink, metal mess.

As she lifted her gaze from the wreckage, ready to question Norman's taste in transportation, something grabbed her attention in the side-mirror. A pick-up truck was coming up behind them, replete with a gun rack and badly painted Confederate flags on the grill. It swerved all over the highway.

She saw that it was filled with good ol' boys, hooting and hollering while staring pointedly at the duo. One appeared to load a rifle, and, with that subtle suggestion, it was time to leave.

Zoe hauled Norman into the passenger seat. With a stomp of her stilt, the car sent the pair careening away from the truck. Zoe pressed down on the gas, steered into the passing lane and glanced over at her new passenger. He was reaching around, trying to find something to grab onto. Just before she looked away, she could have sworn she saw a tiny, furry head pop in and out of the man's face.

"Okay, mister, I didn't want to leave you in the middle of the road," Zoe stated in her most authoritative voice, "but if you have some kind of head parasite, you'd better come clean."

Norman was starting to become lucid. "Am I in a car?" he asked.

Zoe glared. "No, it's a boat."

Norman reached his hand outside the car and dangled his fingers.

"Stop it! You're going to tear your knuckles off!" She grabbed Norman's arm to restrain him. "Yes, it's a car. What were you doing on the highway? Can you...are you allowed to ride a bike? I mean..." She wasn't quite sure how to phrase the question. "What's wrong with your eyes?"

"I lost them in an accident," Norman stated, haltingly. "I'd rather not talk about it."

"I saw something move," she said.

"I...sneezed."

Zoe slowed her car down a bit, just in case she had to leap to safety. "I didn't hear you sneeze."

"Earlier," Norman said. "You've read that nobody can sneeze and keep their eyes open? This is what happens when you try it."

"Do you need to go to a hospital?"

"I'd rather keep this between us."

They drove for a few minutes in silence. Finally, Zoe spoke.

"Sorry about your bike. Can I drop you off somewhere? I'm on my way out of town." She reached down and tugged at one of her stilts.

"Actually, I'm on my way out of town, too. I don't suppose you're going my way?"

"Which way is that?"

Norman was unsure of exactly how to answer that question. Both of them fidgeted while they thought their respective situations through:

Zoe looked over Norman, starting at his head and working downward. *He can't really hurt me, can he? I mean, he's blind. I could outrun him. Hide from him. Probably even outfight him. Unless he's got a gun hidden in his coat. Why would a blind man have a gun hidden in his coat? Wouldn't his aim be off? Unless he can aim by sonar, like a bat. Is he Batman? Did I pick up Batman? If he's Batman, he wouldn't be evil, so that's good. Of course, Batman's not an invalid. This guy has buttholes for eyes. What if they leak? I'm not cleaning up after some blind butthole-leaking mass-murdering rapist.*

Norman was lost inside himself: *Okay, party wolves, can you hear my thoughts? Is there a monitor or something you can look at? I need you to be my eyes. Can you do that? Is there an optic nerve you can stick up your ass, or something? I need ideas. We can't talk out loud, or the cute girl will hear us, and then what do I say? Sorry, lady, I have furry mammals living in my face. Want to help me chase down my eyeballs? Did I just refer to her as cute?*

As he analyzed his new companion, once again he began to see snippets of information via his errant eyeballs: a road sign advertising a motel, and the word "Iowa." They were moving fast. He needed to catch up. He wondered if this strange, cute woman would take him to Iowa.

Zoe, however, was considering her oncoming bout with a violent sociopath. With Walter after her, it might be good to have company. Norman wasn't exactly muscular, and was blind, but, if necessary, she could use him as a human shield. Plus, he was kind of cute, for a blind, butt-eyed potential human shield.

"West!" Norman piped up.

"Okay!" Zoe shot back.

An awkward silence hung in the air as they kept driving. The noonday sun rose higher and higher, looming in the expanse of Midwest sky.

Chapter Eight

"Do you hear something?" Norman asked Zoe.

She cocked an eyebrow. "What do you mean?"

"I think someone is coming up, real fast."

"Let me worry about driving. You can't see the—" Before she could finish, she glanced into her rear-view mirror and saw the same pick-up as before, speeding up to catch them.

"Oh shitting hell!"

"What's that?" asked Norman.

"Nothing. Keep down." Zoe pressed harder on the pedal. She was starting to pull ahead, watching the truck swerve back and forth and accelerate. Someone had raised a skull and bones flag emblazoned with "Liberals Get Out."

Having the muscle car gave Zoe and Norman all the advantages. The rednecks couldn't keep up. "Victory!" Zoe shouted, middle finger raised. Unfortunately, her message was poorly received. She watched as the passengers began throwing junk out the windows.

Several empty bottles, a rocking chair and what looked to be a dead deer were dumped callously into the road. The chair bounced a couple of times before coming to rest in the middle of the highway, causing a semi-truck behind them to jackknife and roll sideways.

A fireball engulfed the rear-view; flames arose from liquid oozing from the semi's cargo container. A heat wave washed down the road, and Norman turned toward Zoe questioningly, even though he could not see her face.

"Sunspots," she whimpered, as the truck roared faster onward.

A full-sized keg came rolling out the driver's side door, accompanied by a loud hoot. The driver's toothy grin quickly changed to a grimace of terror though, as the keg bounced under the right rear tire, sending the truck into a ditch at eighty miles per hour. Debris exploded from the rolling vehicle and cascaded to the ground.

Zoe pulled hard to the right to avoid a large hunk of metal; the car skidded and flopped onto its side. Sparks sprayed Norman's upper body and singed off his eyebrows. He screamed. Gradually, the car came to a halt.

Through blurred, hazy eyes, Zoe saw a horizon where the sky was on the floor and twisted metal and flames were on the ceiling. She unbuckled her safety belt and fell onto her shoulder with a grunt. They were mired in a ditch at the side of the highway. An expanse of green grass, tiny flowers and weeds, and a smattering of car parts and garbage stretched out around them.

"Am I dead?" asked Norman.

"No, just ugly." Zoe unbelted Norman and pulled him out from underneath the vehicle. "Walter always said this thing could handle a grenade. I guess he was right."

"Walter?" Norman tried to right himself. He was sore enough to warrant at least two handfuls of pills, provided his luggage was intact.

"Someone I borrowed the car from," said Zoe, hesitantly.

"Can we get to the luggage?"

"Let me see." Zoe moved toward the scraped-up hunk of steel. Nearby, the flames were starting to spread. "Norman? Back away," she said. "Just crawl backwards. Don't stop until I tell you."

He began doing so as Zoe reached into the rear of the car. Her arm stretched and twisted over the wrecked seats, but she couldn't quite grasp the handles of the bags. The flames now followed a little trail of fluid toward the car.

"Can I stop yet?" Norman called out. Zoe didn't answer, so he continued to feel his way backward, down farther into the ditch and up the other side.

With a sudden burst of agility, Zoe spun around, using her ass as a pivot point, and stuck her leg—stilt and all—into the wreck. The extra three feet of reach allowed her to touch both bags. Ahead, the trail of liquid glimmered in the light of the small fire; it continued its advance.

Only a moment passed before Zoe remembered what was in Walter's trunk. Frantically, she flopped her leg around, trying to catch it on a strap, a handle, anything but a flat surface.

Norman, meanwhile, was starting to get concerned. He had crawled almost fifty feet, and still had heard no "stop" command. He cursed as his knee came down on a rock, and he collapsed in the dirt.

"Crawl! Crawl!" Zoe yelled to Norman, as she focused

31

her energy on retrieving the bags. Inside Walter's trunk, there were several keg sized-barrels of concentrated super-lard. She reached for the glove box and popped it open, stuffing a small pouch of super-lard into her purse for safekeeping. This was the good stuff, a pure and powerful substance that Walter's cult manufactured in their genetics labs. Unfortunately, it was incredibly flammable.

Norman heard her cries from afar and hesitated. If there was danger, he wanted to help, so he set back out the way he came, trying to find Zoe by echolocation.

Zoe reeled back and kicked the luggage with her stilt. The luggage moved closer to the other side of the car. One more thrust, and then all their stuff sat in the ditch. She scrambled awkwardly around the car, just as the edge of the flame slithered up the detached bumper and was swallowed by the trunk. Dragging the bags behind her, she ran away wildly.

Norman crawled toward her with a determined look.

"What the hell are you doing?" she cried.

His face lit up with confusion. "I thought you were in trouble?"

Zoe dove over Norman, the bags slamming into and knocking him down. A moment later, the relative quiet was broken by a roaring crackle. A blast of heat followed, prickling their skin. The entire car was in flames. Thick clouds of black smoke poured from it.

"Do you smell ham?" asked Norman, sniffing the air.

* * *

Minutes later, Zoe and Norman sat in the ditch, listening to the spitting and popping of the super-lard on the road. Norman was trying to concentrate on seeing something—anything. Zoe wished she were blind. She stared at the wreck of Walter's car, aware that she had just committed her most severe, and perhaps final, crime against him.

"We have to go," they both said at once. Awkward, fake laughter followed.

"So, it's unanimous," said Norman. "Any ideas?"

"Well, there's some unpleasantness I'm trying to get away from. I'm starting a new life."

Norman looked glum. "I'm sort of doing that, too. Only it wasn't really my decision."

Zoe regarded the stretch of pavement. A vast, empty plain lay before them. Whether the time of day was a factor or they had just chosen a sparsely traveled highway, no rescue was in sight. She moved closer to Norman. "Whatever happens, it looks like we're going to be here awhile."

Suddenly, they heard a motor rumbling in the distance. A cloud of dust was rolling up the highway, traversing the shoulder of the road. A brick red sedan emerged from the haze. The driver's head barely poked over the dash, and was obscured by a trucker hat. Swallowing a twinge of guilt at what she was about to try, Zoe scrambled across the ground.

"Norman, quick, lay down and look hurt." As he did, Zoe positioned herself in the path of the old car. "Oh God, someone, please!" she shouted. "My ankle!"

Norman began to sit up, a look of concern on his face. Zoe reached a leg over and kicked him back down.

"Shhh! Just be ready when I give the signal," she said.

The car rolled to within a few feet of Zoe's stilts before shuddering to a stop. Leaving the engine running, the driver opened the door and hopped out. He was no more than five feet tall, a shrunken, elderly man with deep carved wrinkles covering every inch of exposed skin.

"A'yup. Need some help, there, friend?" The little man had a hunched way of walking that reminded Zoe of a turtle trying to touch its toes, but he was surprisingly quick. He stood over her, barely taller than she was where she sat, rubbing her stilts.

"My friend and I had a little accident." Zoe pointed to the smoldering heap of steel in the road.

"A'yup. Looks like quite a bender there, that's for sure. My name's Amos Droop." He held out his hand. "You all right?"

"I twisted my ankle, and my friend has a few bumps and bruises, but I think we'll be okay. But the car! Do you think it can be fixed?"

"I reckon we should get you checked out, just in case." The little man placed his hands on his hips and surveyed the wreckage. "Boy, that's quite a crash."

Zoe watched the man as he peered at the stream of burning car parts. Slowly, she got to her feet and tapped Norman's arm. "All my insurance information is stuffed into the driver's side door," she said. "Could you be a lamb and retrieve it for me?"

The door was jammed up against a small tree on the other side of the highway. Though the road was otherwise empty, the little man looked both ways before he began to cross it. "I reckon I can get that for you. Door seems okay. A'yup. Looks like you lucked out."

"Now!" Zoe yelled. She got up and scrambled toward the sedan. Norman grabbed the edge of her sleeve and plunged forward with her.

At the centerline, the little man rotated to see Norman and Zoe jump into his car and lock the doors. "Hey now, friend, what are you—?"

Zoe slammed down the gas pedal, and the sedan peeled away. Rolling down the window, she called out to the confused little man. "Sorry! So sorry!"

Amos Droop watched his sedan recede into the distance. He shook his head and clicked his tongue. "Kids." He waved at the distant silhouette. "You run around on that ankle, it'll get worse! A'yup!" Looking around, he wondered how he was going to get home, then shrugged and began to whistle.

* * *

Zoe felt terrible about stealing poor Amos Droop's car, but knew that they needed to leave town before a metric ton of fury came smashing down on her.

Norman tapped her shoulder gently. "Did we just steal a car?"

"We'll find a way to make this right, somehow," said Zoe, but she wasn't sure if she was trying to convince Norman or herself. "Right now, we have to make up for lost time."

Norman sat back and breathed deeply. He tried to distract himself from his guilt with the images coming through via his eyeballs. They were faded like pages from a fax machine running out of ink, but they were there. He saw miles of road, some signs, buildings, and large, roadside concrete animals. Slowly, a path began to emerge, and he made mental notes of each object he saw. As they drove, he hoped Zoe would spot something that would seem familiar to him, and then he would come barreling down on his eyeballs with all the fury of hell itself.

Chapter Nine

Walter was not happy. He hated driving rental cars. He had not pulled himself up from the morass of his ethnic background only to end up a low-class, downtrodden animal. Walter knew he was better than that.

He had woken up to the sound of his beloved car leaving without him in it, and although he'd only seen tail lights out the window, he would put down money that his bitch had been behind the wheel. This caused him great distress and made his whiskers fall out. Already, he had found two on his chest since departing. He felt less manly, and that was one thing Walter took pride in above all else: He was the manliest walrus in the known world. Manlier than most men, and with the added benefits of his walrus strength and durability, he was a force of nature.

But things had not been going well since he'd left the CBW compound with Zoe. They should have stayed on the grounds, Walter kept telling her. They had plenty to eat, people who understood them, and, legally, she was his property. Plus, they had all the lard she could slather him with.

Walter and Zoe had met when she was in college. Back then, Zoe was a small town girl moving to a new place without her parents, knowing almost nobody. She had always been a little different, due to her feet, so she had learned that she needed to be very careful getting into relationships. She was the girl in class who never took off her stilts. She towered over men, which made dancing awkward. Women assumed she was trying to show off and thus turned the fury of their passive-aggressive bombs on her. She was a nice girl, attractive and smart, sensual and interesting, but she stood a foot or two over everyone else and had trouble finding sensible shoes. A slight odor, not unlike a grocer's freezer section, followed her everywhere she went. This had the unfortunate effect of keeping her from getting to know many people, even casually.

Zoe was walking on campus after class one day when the CBW was on the grounds, passing out pamphlets. Walter was more muscular back then; he had since piled on quite a bit of blubber. Zoe had caught the young walrus's eye, and Walter had immediately begun barking like a seal to catch her attention. It took only a few awkward minutes of small talk for Walter to drop his defenses and ask Zoe out for a fish sandwich and a glass of tartar sauce.

That weekend, the Outreach Program of the Buttered Walrus (OPBW) had hosted a sock-hop. Her fear of being unable to wear socks almost stopped her, but there was something about the way Walter looked at her, so she put anxiety aside and attended the dance. By the end of the night, they were trapped in each other's embrace, making out openly on the dance floor at the local VFW club. Right away, the two became a power couple, even leading the Youth Group of the Buttered Walrus (YGBW) for a time, and becoming involved in the Lubricant Merchandising Department of the Buttered Walrus (LMDBW).

Walter found the nostalgia painful as he drove on in silence. He had tried listening to the radio for a bit, but it pissed him off, so he had ripped it from the rental car and thrown it out the driver's side window.

He remembered the ceremonial masks the humans wore, savage and primitive. Menstrual blood, saliva, semen, ambergris, all colors of bile and more were represented in special jars that had been placed around the room. Beside those small, symbolic containers, huge barrels of super-lard waited for the master of ceremonies to begin the chant, and once he did, Walter had barreled straight to the center of the circle, shoving other walruses and hurling humans into the air. His focus was on Zoe, and when the two met, he with skin shiny and quivering, she with fists dripping with grease, the magic was indescribable. She slathered his belly and rode walrus-back for hours.

Walter rolled down a window, checking the air. The scent was faint, but unmistakably hers, and he pushed the needle past its limit. Every second that she put distance between them, the odor of her secret parts would fade, leaving Walter without a map.

He would not allow that to happen.

* * *

Farther down the road, the eyeballs had finally found a place to stop: The Motel Sick.

Hazel had gone inside the motel to see if she could wrangle a room, leaving Azul on guard duty. The clerk, snoring and sputtering, was in the midst of deep sleep.

"Hey!" Hazel yelled. "Hey you!"

The clerk woke up long enough to see an eyeball standing on the counter in front of him. He assumed he was dreaming, but when the eyeball dragged a wad of money over the edge of the counter and deposited it underneath the clerk's nose, he perked up.

"We need a room. For two, please," Hazel said.

The clerk stared down through sleepy eyes, blinking and fingering the crust at the edges. At the Motel Sick, no drugs were necessary to see and experience weird shit. He shrugged and took the money, somewhere around a dozen twenty dollar bills.

"Room preference?" asked the clerk. Cash meant he didn't give a fuck.

"We require a place of fascinating sights and scenic vistas. A place with nooks and crannies in which we can nest and spin our web of freedom," said the eyeball. "Is this enough money?"

The clerk slid a key across the desk. "Normally, I'd need more, but I like the look of you." He pocketed a wad of cash, peeling off two of the bills and dropping them into the register. He knew exactly what room to give them.

A few minutes later, when the two eyeballs went scrambling across the floor of the lobby and up the stairs, the clerk just looked the other way. He took a long plug from a dark bottle hidden behind the counter, belched, and put his head back down on the desk to nap until the next freaks came by, looking for a room.

* * *

Tooling down the highway in between the angry walrus and the Motel Sick, those freaks were making good time. They had been driving for miles, and neither of them seemed sure of where to go.

Norman felt a sudden yet familiar sensation and knew that something was coming up for air. In a panic, he unbuckled his seatbelt and leaned over the backseat.

"Oh my god, are you gonna throw up?" asked Zoe. "Norman, please don't barf back there. I can stop. Should I stop?"

"No," he said. "Keep going." Pressure grew in his temples. Then there was a pop, and his face gave birth to a small, furry animal. He felt around, his hand brushing across Smitty's back.

"Hey," whispered Smitty. "What's up?"

"What are you doing out here?" Norman also whispered, but angrily.

"We drew straws, and I lost. You need a sniffer who can go the distance; someone with balls." Smitty grabbed his crotch, made a thrusting gesture and laughed like a hyena.

"What the hell is that?" shouted Zoe, craning her head around to try to see the backseat, even as she kept one eye on the road.

"Bark!" said Smitty. He bounced around.

Zoe's eyes widened. "What the hell?"

Norman thought he knew where Smitty was going with this, even if it was a bad idea. "Didn't I mention I had a dog? This is my dog... Smitty." Smitty leapt over the seat back and landed in Norman's lap with a thump, then held out a paw to shake.

Zoe reached out toward the paw, but retracted her hand quickly. "No, no, wait a minute. You did *not* have a dog when I picked you up."

"He's my seeing eye dog," Norman said.

Smitty attempted to hump Zoe's leg. She pushed him off. "But why didn't I see him before?"

Norman wasn't sure what to say, so he went with a stupid, stupid lie.

"He's a stealth seeing-eye dog. They're trained to be virtually invisible."

Zoe looked down at Smitty, who was eyeing her breasts, a long string of drool stretching from his jaw to the seat cushion between Norman and herself. "He's pretty visible now."

"Growl," said Smitty, attempting to wink. It made him look less flirtatious and more like he had a mild case of Tourettes.

"You've heard those stories about dogs who follow their owners across five states when they move?" Norman said. "Smitty here is like that, only he's much faster, so he follows about two car lengths behind me wherever I go."

Zoe seemed ready to open the door and bolt. "Then how is he a seeing eye dog? Shouldn't he stay with you?"

"And here he is!" Norman said, with a tad too much enthusiasm.

38

Zoe studied Norman and Smitty. She considered the contents of her purse: chewing gum, a tampon, nail clippers, lipstick, a mirror, the super-lard she'd retrieved from the glove box—and her personal defense kit. She felt ready, just in case these weirdos turned out to be more dangerous than they seemed.

"Just make him stop looking at my chest," Zoe said, turning both eyes back toward the road. Norman glared at Smitty, but the little party wolf just grinned and let his tongue loll, spattering Norman's jeans with drool that smelled of pot and old socks.

Cooter's calm voice echoed inside Norman's head.

"Sorry about the interruption, bro. We didn't cock-block you, did we?"

"What the hell are you doing?" Norman thought, with all the rage he could muster.

"Dude, you have no idea where you're going; let's face it, you're kind of clueless. Besides, we *want* to help. You're not only our home, you're our bro!"

Smitty now sat in the middle seat, staring at Zoe, licking his balls furiously.

"He's got a good nose, man," said Cooter. "Trust me, when he gets a scent, he's like a radar dish in a hairy little dude's body."

I hope you're not yanking my chain, Cooter." Norman returned his attention to Zoe. "Okay, Zoe, this guy? He's a tracker. He should be able to sniff out somewhere safe."

Smitty jumped up on Norman's lap. He was surprisingly heavy. He pawed at the window, winking at Norman, who rolled it down. Smitty leaned his head over the side and let his fur flap in the breeze. "Wheeeee!" he shouted.

Zoe glanced over again. "Did your dog just say 'whee?'"

Norman raced for answers. "He's got asthma. It was more of a wheeze." He cuffed Smitty on the back of the head. In response, Smitty shifted his weight so that his back legs pressed into Norman's testicles. Norman decided to leave well enough alone and not agitate the little sociopath further.

* * *

The American Midwest was bland and featureless, huge flat patches of earth over which a glacier had rolled over a million years ago, crushing mountains into plains. Occasionally, the expanse of nothingness was broken up by a tree line or small rest stop. As the hours lengthened and the shadows shifted directions, malaise overtook Norman and Zoe. She looked down at the gas meter; it jittered at just below a quarter-tank.

"We should stop and get gas," she said.

"I think I saw a sign a minute ago," Norman drawled, shaking himself fully awake. "The Cum N' Go Gas-stop."

"How could you *see* a sign?"

Norman had to pause for a moment.

"Maybe I dreamed it?" He could have sworn he had seen it. Perhaps his eyes had been there.

"Holy crap, Norman!" Zoe said, a hint of admiration in her voice. "There it is, the Cum N' Go Gas-stop! You nailed it!" They pulled to a stop and Zoe hopped out. "I got it," she said, pulling a card from her purse. Norman was left inside with the party wolves.

Herb's stoned drawl came creeping up from inside Norman. "Ha ha, she thinks you're a dog, dude!"

Smitty turned angry circles in Norman's lap. "Shut up!" he whined.

"We need jerky!" Cooter shouted.

Sophie's voice arose, sweet and lilting. "Norman, we can't run out to the store to fill the fridge, and our usual hunting methods might pose a problem right now. Could you be a sweetheart and get us some supplies?"

Norman sighed. "Okay, okay. What do you want?"

"Sheep!" Herb shouted.

"They're not going to have sheep, you jackass," Rex snarled from somewhere behind Norman's right ear. "It's a convenience store."

"Smitty, go in with him. You know what we like," said Cooter.

Norman popped the door. "Be right back," he said to Zoe.

"Don't be long," she shouted after him.

Once alone, she let out a long sigh. The gas pump clicking away, she reached down to pet her calves over the wraps. "I'm sorry, boys," she said. "I know this sucks. But we have to be careful. People just don't understand. And you know who understands too well. Just a little longer, okay?"

If anyone had been present, they would have heard Zoe's feet honk in response.

* * *

Zoe was sitting in the car, leaning impatiently on the horn, when Norman finally stumbled from the store. In his arms were two bags of processed snacks and caffeinated energy drinks.

Smitty frolicked happily in front of him, like a cartoon character with a huge shit-eating grin. They practically fell into the car, sending a waterfall of snacks onto the floorboard.

"Hungry?" Zoe asked.

"Energy is important on road trips," said Norman. Smitty was already rooting around in the pile, claiming bags of beef jerky and energy shots.

As they pulled back onto the highway, Smitty stuffed some snacks into Norman's face. A bouquet of grasping paws shot out and collected the bags and bottles before retreating into Norman's skull. Zoe glanced over, but all she saw was Norman looking very unhappy, and Smitty on his lap, chewing on cheese curls and drooling orange out the window.

* * *

Less than an hour later, as the shadows grew long, both human passengers were tired, depressed, and not talking about it. Zoe kept thinking about the life she'd left. Her fears that it would catch up with her simultaneously drove her forward and made her want to curl up and sleep until it all went away.

Norman kept wondering where his life had gone so wrong that he was stuck without eyes on a road trip with a strange woman and a bunch of animals living in his face. A part of him wished that Zoe had just run him down when he was on the bike.

They were passing an old billboard advertising some kind of motel when Smitty started going crazy.

"Smitty! Smitty, down!" Norman yelled, but the little party wolf ran circles around the front seat.

"What the hell is he doing? Get him off me!" Zoe screeched, trying to keep the car straight as Smitty barked and whooped and bounced.

The other party wolves howled in Norman's skull, making him jerk forward and slam his head into the windshield.

Cooter's calm voice broke through the chaos. "He's got something, Norman."

Norman seized the wheel. "Turn here!" he yelled.

Zoe slapped his hands away, but followed the exit off the highway and onto the ramp. "What the fuck is wrong with you?" she said. "Don't act like a psychopath!"

41

Thoughts flooded his cerebrum. His eyes had been here. He recognized the images like a series of still photographs, everything from the road signs to the debris off the side of the exit ramp.

"Turn right up here," said Norman through gritted teeth. He imagined strangling his own eyes, or at least giving them a good talking to.

Zoe, exhausted from the day of driving, just wanted to change her foot-wraps. They were starting to fray, and she was a little worried that she'd caught a familiar smell wafting up from near the brake pedal.

The vehicle rounded a corner. In the near distance, a building sat alone against a backdrop of dusky sky. A neon vacancy sign flashed pink and green, sizzling every few cycles and lighting nearby insects on fire. The screams of dying mosquitoes filled the air, too tiny for Norman or Zoe to hear.

Chapter Ten

The parking lot was mostly empty. A few beaten up metal shells rusted under daily blasts of noonday sun. A large yellow sign, the classic 1970's style asymmetrical triangle, stood at the edge of the parking lot. Huge, fading red letters, pitching outward, read: MOTEL SICK. Below that, despite their age, smaller black letters clung tenaciously to a dirty off-white signboard. "Hourly rates. Specialty rooms. Cheap!" the sign beckoned.

Zoe retrieved her bag from the backseat and stepped out of the vehicle. Norman grabbed her outstretched hand and followed. Turning toward the car, he shouted, "Stay, Smitty!" The little party wolf waited until Zoe was inside to flip Norman off.

A tumbleweed blew across the lot as Norman reached the doors. Above them, a torn sign reading "Office" had been modified via black magic marker to read "Orifice." It seemed somehow appropriate.

They stood at the counter, waiting patiently for a clerk. Everything in the lobby featured a thick layer of what could only charitably be called dust. It was the color of snot, and flaky. A few battered couches and a small leather chair faced a television with rabbit ears. These were not antennas, but actual rabbit ears, stuffed and mounted. Several paintings hung on the walls: cheaply framed prints of animals, though not in ordinary nature scenes.

A portrait of aardvarks bowling in an alley: the tiny bowling shirts they wore were adorable. One of them was in the middle of his forward momentum, about to send a ball rumbling toward the pins, but instead of a ball, the aardvark held a human fetus. The umbilical cord receded past the outstretched arm of the aardvark bowler, traveled across the floor of the alley, strewn with beer cans and cigarette butts, and ended up still attached to the mother. She was a woman in a floral 1950's style housedress, eyes both black and puffy, and she was duct taped to the wall. Motel Sick, indeed.

Zoe didn't even look at the pictures. She was busy tapping on the wall of the room behind the desk.

"Hello? We need some service. We have cash!" She winked at Norman, forgetting momentarily that he couldn't see.

"Help you?" a greasy voice sputtered from behind the counter. The clerk stood up from the floor, where he had been napping. He barely looked at Zoe and Norman as he pulled a dusty rate card from behind the counter and used it to brush off some crumbs that were still stuck to him. "Welcome to the Motel Sick," he said. "We have a variety of rooms for you to choose from. I see you're traveling together. He slapped the rate card down in front of them. May I interest you in one of our special rooms for romantical pleasure?"

"Just a regular room," said Norman, sliding up beside Zoe.

The man scratched his asshole through stained sweatpants. "Ain't got no regular rooms. All we got is special rooms. Here, look at the catalog."

Zoe scanned the broadsheet on the counter. Numerous small pictures showed a variety of suites for the discerning fetishist. Each room had a short description and a rate.

"What do you...recommend?" Norman asked.

"We just want something simple," Zoe said.

The clerk pointed to one of the selections. "This one might be right for you. The Irish Potato Famine room. Simple. Down to earth. Room has actual potato blight. You bring a potato anywhere within fifteen feet of that room, it's going to blight, you watch." Noticing a blank look on his customers' faces, he quickly added, "You get all the butter you can eat."

"What else you got?" asked Zoe.

"Well, there's the empty room."

"That sounds fine," said Norman.

The clerk lowered his voice, though nobody else was present. "Just between you and me, you don't want that one. Totally empty. No bed. No dresser. No doors, walls, ceiling. Oh, and you have to be checked out before check-in time."

"Okay..." said Zoe.

"The birdhouse room is nice," the clerk continued. "Features old-world wooden finishing."

"Let me guess," she snarled. "There's a fucking perch in there?"

"What? A perch? That's stupid." The clerk made a face.

"No, there are little holes all over the walls, over five-hundred hand-drilled apertures, so the birds can come and go and fly around the room. It's great for nature lovers."

"What kind of birds?" Zoe asked, suspiciously.

"Oh, sparrows, larks, finches mostly," said the man. "We got one pelican."

She stared down at the sheet. A picture of a snowy field caught her interest. "What's this one?"

The clerk squinted to see where she was pointing. "The Antarctic Room," he answered with a smile. "We keep it at a bone chilling negative fifty-six degrees Fahrenheit. If you're the kind of people who bring ice into the bedroom for a thrill, you'll blow your load on the wall as soon as you walk in."

Zoe slapped some money on the counter. "We'll take it."

Norman was confused. "Wait, what?"

The clerk took the cash and fished around in a box of keys behind the counter. "Don't...you know...actually blow your load on the walls. That was hyperbole. It would freeze, and then the housekeepers would have to chip it off with an ice scraper."

* * *

Zoe led Norman down the hall toward room number 18— the "Antarctic Room"—as he dragged the luggage. He tried to stay aware of his surroundings, just in case the eyeballs made their presence known. He could almost smell them, and it occurred to him that people don't realize their eyes have a smell until that smell is missing.

Zoe ducked underneath a low hanging doorway arch and heard screams coming from her left. A large set of gold numbers on the door marked it as room 11, which, according to the pamphlet she had lifted from the front desk, was "The Screaming Room of Eternal Nightmares." The finest imported screams had been trapped in an air-locked, sonic-filter laden room, constructed with the latest in space age technology and voodoo magic. No matter how many times the sound waves bounced off something, they just kept going. There were screams in there over forty years old.

They finally came to room 18. "Here we are," Zoe said, pulling her sweater around her shoulders. "Hope you brought extra clothes."

"Why do we have to stay in the cold room?" Norman asked.

"You're complaining? I'm paying for it. Come on, it'll

45

be fun." She opened the door. An icy blast blew over them. Through the door, a small yurt with a flag atop it was visible. Apparently, the yurt was the Antarctic Room's version of a canopy bed. Norman dropped the luggage to the floor, which was like permafrost.

"Check this out," Zoe said. Norman heard her turn on the shower. "Says on the handle that the water is heated to just above thirty-eight degrees, enough to keep it from freezing but not enough to actually be warm. Amazing, huh?"

"Do we get Sherpas?" asked Norman.

She looked over the wastes, thought about her feet and shivered. They would be very happy here. She put her suitcases next to the bed and looked around. Other than the tent/bed there wasn't much to the room. Just arctic winds and bleak, barren landscapes rife with entropy.

"Hey Zoe, you go ahead and get comfortable. I'm going to poke around. I know this sounds weird, but I have a feeling there's something here that'll help me find my eyes."

"Let's go then," she said. "I don't want you stumbling into the wrong room."

Norman smiled. He would have to remember to thank her profusely when this was over.

* * *

Back in the lobby, the clerk was already asleep. Zoe led Norman to the counter, tapping her fingers next to the clerk's head. It only seemed to make him snore louder.

Zoe glanced at the picture next to the front desk, which read "Our Founder": a grotesque, round man sitting in a chair, bending over toward his feet. He was straining, sinews of skin pulling apart like silly putty as he leaned over to take a bite out of his own foot. She hoped this was not indicative of the continental breakfast.

"Have you seen a couple of eyeballs come through here?" Norman asked.

With a snort, the clerk forced open his eyes. He looked at them silently for a moment and blinked, slowly.

"I'm sorry. It's the policy of the Hotel Sick not to divulge information on any possible guests who may or may not have stayed in our facilities in the past, present or future," he said.

There was another long moment of silence.

The clerk cleared his throat. "So...that's our policy." He stared at Norman for a long time, the only sound the ticking of a wall clock behind the desk.

Zoe also cleared her throat, loudly. It sounded like she was hacking the word, "Norman."

He turned. "What?"

"Money," she said. "Give him money."

The clerk just stared. Norman's pulled a couple of bills from his pocket and passed them over the counter.

"Thank you, sir." The clerk's grin looked greasy. "But as I said, the official policy of Motel Sick disallows any and all information given out about our guests." The man twitched like he'd just been stung by a wasp. Then he tapped on the desk. Zoe looked down; a dirty fingernail hovered beside a small picture of a room at the hotel: The Panopticon.

Chapter Eleven

Inside the Panopticon, there was no ceiling. Giant gray clouds rolled overhead, shifting and changing form. Occasional bursts of thunder rumbled, making the room vibrate. The floor was a long, steel walkway, polished to a gleaming shine, with large metal bolts holding pieces together between deep-cut seams. A thin railing kept anyone from falling over the edge of the walkway.

In the middle was a huge ring, at least a mile in circumference. It circled around a white stone tower in the center. A stretch of dirt between the walkway and the central tower deepened as it crept toward the tower's base.

The door through which they entered was the only part of that wall not covered in mirrors. The covering had the effect of making the room appear much larger, more disorienting. In the tower, a number of opaque glass sections rimmed the uppermost section.

Norman pushed against one of the nearby mirrored panels. To his surprise, it slid aside, revealing a coat closet.

"You don't think they're all like this, do you?" Zoe said. She stepped toward another mirror and tapped on it. A hollow thump answered her, so she slid the mirror aside to expose a mini-fridge, stocked with little bottles of liquors and expensive-looking chocolates.

Norman sighed. "Why even bother? I can't see. I can't think. I give up."

"That's stupid," Zoe said. "At least you're doing something instead of just waiting around to die."

He hung his head. "If you hadn't let me come along, I wouldn't have even made it this far. How am I going to check all this space? If every mirror slides, that could mean a hundred little rooms. I don't know where to start!"

"We'll start right here, and we'll each go around in the opposite direction. You feel; I'll look." Zoe smiled. "By the time we meet up, we'll have found...well, something. Okay?"

Norman was in awe. A huge wave of affection crashed over him. He needed to come clean. It was the least she deserved.

"Zoe?" he asked. "Can I tell you something weird?"

"Sure, go ahead."

"It's about what I'm looking for. You may have noticed that I can't see."

"You're missing your eyes. It's okay, I figured it out awhile back, but don't sweat it. I had a boyfriend in high school with only one testicle. He lost the other when he hit a ramp on his bike and the seat came off before he landed the jump. Slid down his leg like a soggy water balloon."

"Jesus... But, well, okay. The thing is," sputtered Norman, trying to think happy thoughts, "they have minds of their own."

Zoe stared. "Go on."

"They escaped. They ran off together. I think I can get them back. Or something like that. I just need to figure out where they've gone. I know I sound insane, but trust me, there's no better way to tell you what's been happening to me. Will you help me look for clues?"

"What kind of clues?"

"Anything that seems like it was left here accidentally. Maps, ticket stubs, notes, you know. They probably looked for somewhere to hide. They're used to being inside a couple of holes barely bigger than they are, so search for nooks and crannies."

And, with that, they began making circles around the monolithic Panopticon.

* * *

The Panopticon was without clocks, and the sky never seemed to change. It was perpetual twilight, a gathering storm on the horizon, not quite breaking but always threatening to dump its contents on the room below.

Zoe moved across the expanse, navigating along the wall, walking tall on her stilts and having to bend very carefully to check anything beneath the three-foot level. As she disappeared behind the tower, Norman heard a chorus of growls and groans.

As his face began to distort, he dropped to his knees and jammed a hand into his mouth to keep from crying out. Within seconds, Cooter and Herb stood before him. Herb, smoking an enormous blunt, was giggling to himself.

"What's up, Norman Spooter?" Cooter stuck a paw out and grabbed Norman's hand, putting it through a series of changing grips and gestures. When the hipster handshake was complete, Cooter waited expectantly.

Norman glared at the party wolf. "What are you doing out here?"

"Man, she's way over on the other side. We've got time to kill. How can I help?"

"The eyeballs have been here. I know it. Help me look for clues?"

Herb sucked smoke from his fatty. "Clues..." he snickered.

"You gonna give me a Cooter snack?" asked Cooter, grinning, which sent Herb into another fit of hysterics.

"Damn it, you guys," growled Norman. "This is serious. You gotta help me out."

Herb blew a ring of smoke. "Where's Smitty?"

"We left him in the car."

"Aw man." Herb looked very sad. "He's gonna eat all the snacks."

"He's the best sniffer, too," said Cooter, grinning a sly grin.

A growl came from inside Norman's head: "You ladies in or out?" It was the unmistakable buzzsaw baritone of Rex.

"Deal me in," said Herb. "Hold 'em, hold 'em, hold 'em!" Cooter started toward the entrance, but Norman's outstretched arm stopped him.

"Come on, Norman," he said. "I'm winning."

"Listen. If you don't do something useful for me right now, I'm going to throw myself off the roof of this place, and I'm going to make sure I do it headfirst." The expression on Norman's face, eyes or no, told Cooter that he wasn't joking.

"Okay, okay," the party wolf acquiesced. "Judging from the size of this circle, we got about ten minutes until she comes around the other side of that tower and sees us."

"I need ideas," said Norman. "If you were an eyeball, and you were hiding from the authorities, where would you hole up?"

Cooter said nothing, but was off like a shot, doing his best to imitate his cousins, the bloodhounds. The party wolf ran from mirror to mirror. He caught the reflection of the tower in one of them. Its windows were covered in slats and shaded heavily, obscuring the interior even to Cooter's sharp eyes. The idea that there could be someone in there seeing them but remaining unseen was unsettling.

Norman, holding onto the Party Wolf's tail, reached over and pushed on the nearest mirror. It opened into a bedroom. "Nothing. Just a bunch of boring stuff," Cooter growled. He was moving fast from door to door now, and the party wolf went into a pointing pose in front of one of the mirrors. The mirror shuddered as it squeaked open, revealing a small bathroom, tidy and clean.

"What?" Norman whispered.

"I smell something in here," said Cooter.

It looked like a generic hotel bathroom, but, stepping through the mirror-door, Norman's hand grazed a high-tech hinge that was attached to its top.

"What do you think this is?" he asked.

Cooter shrugged.

When Norman pulled the hinge, a small whirring noise started up, like a dentist's drill, and, before he could react, the mirror slid and flipped so that the translucent inside was now on the outside. With sickening gravity, he realized that the mirrors were designed so that who or whatever was in the tower could see through every mirror-door in the room with a single touch. It was a privacy junkie's worst nightmare.

Norman sank to the floor. "I give up, Cooter. I feel like crying, but don't know if I can."

"You still have tear ducts, right?"

As Norman absent-mindedly brushed his fingers across the floor, his thumb traveled through a drop of something wet. About a foot past the first drop he found a second, and a third a few feet later.

"Look at this," Norman said. Cooter bent down next to him, sniffing.

"It's not water; not pee," said Cooter. "And it's only here in the bathroom."

Norman stuck a finger into one of the droplets and brought it to his nose. The slight medicinal scent, mixed with purified water and a lubricant was unmistakable: eye drops.

Cooter turned his canine grin toward Norman. "Hey landlord," he said, cheerfully. "What thing do you think is most important to eyeballs?"

"Seeing?" suggested Norman. Then it hit him. His thoughts rolled over the horizon to the imposing monument to prison fantasies at the center of the room. Of course the eyeballs wouldn't want anyone spying on them. They were in a precarious position, being as fragile as grapes and lacking any real defenses. They would want a place where they could observe their environment—the central tower.

51

"Good boy, Cooter! Quick, get into my skull! Let's go tell Zoe."

* * *

Zoe was enjoying the weather. Her feet aside, the rising storm was a nice break from the chilly Panopticon. She looked out over the yard at the tower. Just then, Norman came lurching up to her, panting and out of breath.

"We need to get out to the tower," he said. "Any ideas?"

Zoe contemplated things for a few moments. "It looks like it's off limits. There's no bridge, no rope ladder, no signs of a secret passage." She frowned at the endless mirrored panels that made up the impossibly obfuscated tower. Then, suddenly, she started running back and forth from the panels to the railing at the edge of the walkway.

"What are you doing?" Norman asked.

"Shhh, I'm warming up. Get out of the way." Gently, Zoe pushed Norman backwards. As he stumbled to the side, she bent down and whispered to her bandaged feet.

"Okay, boys, ready?"

Standing up, she rocketed forward, pounding her legs like pistons. Zoe hit the edge of the platform, took a quick step up onto the railing and leapt high into the air.

She moved her stilts with precision, and, as she flew, her legs seemed to glide. Zoe caught one of the glass window panels with the edges of her fingers. As she slammed against the tower, the panel into which she crashed split in two.

Nothing moved until a piece of wood—just long to fit over the gap between the tower and the walkway around it—emerged from the darkness. Stamped on top was "Property of Motel Sick Maintenance." At the other end, Zoe stood, smiling broadly. She seemed to have a case of happy-feet, as she was doing a little dance and whispering "shhh" to herself.

"Norman, in front of you is a board," she called out. "I need you to cross it very carefully."

Sitting and scooting across on his butt like a toddler, he did just that.

Inside the tower was a small control room, dim, dusty and obviously used for storage. Soap, shampoo, towels, notepads and tiny Bibles had been stacked or folded atop one another or put in boxes.

Zoe looked down at a small device that blinked angrily. "This must be for a hidden door," she said. "The maids wouldn't want to long jump every time they needed to replace a toilet paper roll."

"How did you do that?" Norman asked, still in awe, standing and dusting himself off.

She blushed. "Maybe later. Let's look for your eyeballs."

There was a surveillance area set up on a rotating base. A tall desk, with several telescope-like devices jutting from it, sat in front of a stool and some levers. If this had been used to spy on people in the past, it wasn't now, but then that was the point of the Panopticon: you never knew whether or not you were being watched.

"Of course they'd be in here," Norman said. "They would want to keep an eye out for me."

Zoe stared at the stool. It was gigantic—seven feet off the floor at seat level. A layer of dust sat thick upon its surface. In the dust, there was a silhouette where something had disturbed the layer, and a few wet, sticky droplets. Her stilts allowed her to see across the top, so she walked over for a closer look.

She plucked a scrap of paper from the top of the stool. The handwriting on it was terrible. It was definitely written without the benefit of thumbs. Hastily scrawled as it was, the note clearly read "Tagus—Twin Spheres" above an address.

"Tagus, North Dakota," Zoe said, matter-of-factly. "That's where they're headed."

Norman's eyeholes opened wide. "What? How do you know?"

"I found a note. Besides, don't you read the news? Tagus is the number one cult and weirdo destination in the world for marriage licensing. They'll marry anything, even a woman and a walrus."

Norman furrowed his brow. "What?"

"Nothing," said Zoe, quickly. "Anyway, the point is they'd marry people, animals..."

He frowned. "Or two eyeballs."

"Definitely."

"That must be their plan! We have to stop them!"

"Relax, Norman. They can't move too fast. Every one of your steps is, like, thirty of theirs. Let's sleep for a few hours, then we'll take off and catch up to them before they even get to Tagus."

"But—"

Stepping up to Norman, Zoe pressed her body against his in a much-needed hug. "It's going to be okay," she said.

Immediately, Zoe began thinking thoughts that made

her feel guilty. She knew they stemmed, in part, from her flight from Walter, and her tendency to rebound from serious relationships involving giant pinnipeds. Some, though, seemed to come from a place where she realized—to her horror—that she really liked Norman.

As they left the Panopticon, she held his hand, his arm angled up slightly to compensate for her stilts. A part of Norman wanted to beat down depression by taking her to bed; another part was too scared to even consider this. Sexual tension rising, they walked in silence back to the Antarctic Room and shut the door behind them.

Chapter Twelve

Hazel and Azul had checked out early. The excitement of their impending wedding had made them both too giddy to sleep, even with the vast expanse of the Panopticon to lull them into visual intoxication. They had found their way into its tower through a drainpipe. Sometimes it helped to be small.

As they lay on top of their stool, pouring over marriage brochures and whispering sweet nothings to each other, the storm outside—or, perhaps, in an adjacent room—began to deliver a light rain. Azul snuggled up to Hazel, and they listened to the drops for a while before Azul spoke.

"Alas, my faithful companion and life partner, I cannot sleep."

"What's the matter, my love?"

"Well, for one thing, I cannot close myself."

"Neither can I."

So, electric with anticipation, they decided to press on without sleep. Hazel suggested a grueling pace.

* * *

Hours later, they sat on a rust-eaten swing set in an abandoned city park in the tiny town of Tagus. They hadn't seen a single person since entering town, although a curtain would occasionally flutter inside a house, or something colorful would flash between buildings. There were people here, but no set of instructions to explain how to contact them.

"What do we do now?" asked Azul. "How do we find our liberators?"

Hazel was afraid to tell her sweet, naive Azul that she didn't know. She had been the de facto leader of the duo since they'd begun plotting their escape, but her plans hadn't taken her quite this far.

"We must be strong, comrade," she said, doing her best

impression of Karl Marx. "For we are right, and we are mighty, and furthermore, we are..."

As Azul waited for her to finish, a long shadow fell over them. Two hands, tattooed with symmetrical runic designs, reached out and seized them roughly, plunging both eyes into darkness.

* * *

Back at the Motel Sick, Norman and Zoe stood shivering in the arctic wind.

"Only one bed," Zoe said. "Looks like we're sharing."

"Yeah," Norman gulped.

"We'll want to leave early, I guess. Try to make up time."

Norman felt awkward getting undressed. He waited until Zoe had retired to the bathroom before unbuttoning his pants and getting into bed. Placing the sheet between himself and the mattress, he squirmed out of the last of his clothing.

When she entered the tent, Zoe stood before Norman in a slinky, fur-lined camisole with matching panties. She'd placed two large velvet sacks over her stilts.

"So, I guess you're joining me, huh?" she asked, coyly.

"I wasn't... I mean..." Norman regained control over his tongue. "It's cold."

Zoe clicked off the light switch. "It *is* cold." With that, she took a running leap into the bed. The mattress bounced; frosted springs creaked and swore as they rocked. Zoe slipped under the covers and lay there silently. Norman listened to her breathe.

Suddenly, he felt her move against his body.

"Can I warm my feet up on you?" she asked.

"Of course." Norman pulled his legs up and placed them back under the sheet. Afraid to say anything more, lest the awkward seduction stop, he waited silently, feeling her slide her feet upward until the stilts were lodged between his thighs. Whatever was underneath those stilts was very large, and he imagined Zoe as a Sasquatch, stomping through the wilderness in lingerie.

Zoe's feet were beginning to get comfortable, and she knew that soon they would start moving on their own accord. She made her decision: she was going to tell Norman about her anatomical anomaly.

Before she could open her mouth, he said something that surprised them both.

"Can I kiss you?"

She paused for only a moment, then: "Don't ask me. Just do it."

Norman put his arms around Zoe and held her close. Their lips found one another.

"Is this okay?" he whispered to her.

"Norman, I think I need this," she whispered back.

Zoe slipped her hands into his pants; he unclasped her bra. Zoe sighed and rubbed her body against Norman's. He traced her form with his fingertips until he reached the stilts. He started to undo the ribbon that tied the bag on her right foot, but she stiffened and pulled him back up to pillow-level.

"I was just—"

Zoe put a finger to his lips and rolled him onto his back. Several intimate minutes later, Norman felt her place a condom on his penis.

"No latex allergies, right?" She giggled.

He squeaked out a "no" as her hand guided him inside of her. They fell into an easy rhythm. Zoe's breathing became shallower, but more rapid. As Norman melted into Zoe's body, he heard a faint noise accompanying each squeak of the bedsprings. It sounded like muffled honking.

Squeak.
Breathe.
Honk.

SQUEAK.
BREATHE.
HONK.

They were reaching climax, convulsing against one another. Zoe ground her hips into Norman's. He needed to scream, and, as he cried out, the bed gave one final gasp. Underneath it all, Norman heard a long and unsettling "SQUAWWWWK!" It reminded him of being at the beach, when he would look for seagulls and chase them down the sand.

He pulled out suddenly, jumped from the bed. "Did you hear that?"

"Get back here!" Zoe shouted. "We're not done!"

Norman tried to unstick the bed frame from the icy floor. "I think there's an animal under here."

Zoe frowned. "Norman, come back. It's nothing to

worry about. I coughed, and I sound like an osprey when I cough."

"It sounded like it was coming from somewhere else," he insisted.

"I can throw my voice...and cough, okay. Just get back to bed."

Norman was irritated. The combination of the freezing weather, the sudden shock of animal noises and the interruption of sex had shrunk him to the size of a coat button.

Zoe looked down at his depressed wiener. "It's okay," she said.

He returned to bed. "I'm sorry."

"Don't worry about it. Life's a journey, not a destination."

Norman blushed, again, as Zoe settled her head on his chest.

"I'm not very experienced. I'm sorry."

"Maybe when this is all over, we'll give it another shot."

He put his arm around her shoulders and pulled her close. Norman heard her begin to snore, and less than a minute after Zoe, he was asleep, too.

* * *

BLAM!

Norman?" Zoe said, shaking him.

BLAM!

He awoke with a start, his body revolting against being jarred out of REM sleep. His brain felt full of cotton candy. The inside of his mouth tasted like a wet cat.

BLAM!

He hopped out of bed and opened the tent flap.

BLAM!

The door rocked it on its frost-laden hinges. Glass and plaster fell, so much so that it seemed the wall might come down first.

"This must be part of the room's charm," said Norman. "Maybe it's, like, the buffeting winds of the Antarctic? Should I call down and have them turn it off?"

BLAM!

"There must be a mechanism. Hold on."

"Be careful, Norman," Zoe cautioned.

He bent down to feel the wood, eager to satisfy his curiosity. At that moment, the smashing sound stopped. "See? It's on a timer. Nothing to worry about."

A loud *crack*, then two long sabers smashed through the

wall, gouging pits inches from where Norman's head had been seconds before.

A look of terror flashed in Zoe's eyes. "Norman!" she screamed, then ran for her clothes.

Chapter Thirteen

Through the plaster and beyond the ivory spikes, wrinkled gray skin glistened in the pale hallway light. The spikes retracted, plaster crumbling around the gaping holes, before they smashed through the wall again. A crack spread from floor to ceiling.

"It's an assassin!" Norman screamed, dressing hurriedly. "He's got swords!"

"I'll explain later," Zoe said. "Right now we have to—"

"I know you're in there, bitch!" came a grumbling shout. "Leave now and I won't eat your little friend!"

"Eat me?"

Zoe shrieked, "We have to go, now!"

The wall took yet another heavy blow. This time, their attacker miscalculated and hit a stud. His tusks were stuck fast.

Zoe grabbed Norman's hand and yanked him toward the window overlooking the courtyard. Slipping on the icy floor, he tried to keep up with her.

"What are you—?" was all he had time to say before he was yanked through the glass, shards flying everywhere. Warm air hit them like a breath. It felt good, though it did little to stave off Norman's fear of an impending demise.

"Go limp!" Zoe shouted, and they hit the ground together, their bodies barely cushioned by a bed of overgrowth and refuse. Norman's organs shuddered from the impact. He would definitely need a handful of random pills after this.

Zoe picked herself up quickly. "We need to get to the car," she whispered. "Right now."

Grasping Norman's middle and index fingers, she pulled him along. The pressure around his digits was warm and comforting. He floated along behind Zoe as she opened the door to the lobby.

They got less than ten feet into the parking lot when a thunderous roar echoed across it.

On the balcony above, a nightmarish shape loomed, silhouetted against the full moon. A misshapen trapezoid of a head sat atop broad, hunched shoulders, heaving with rage. Hideous flippers grazed the banister, then rose up and came smashing down on the railing, twisting the metal into the aftermath of a demolition derby. Moonlight caught two gleaming tusks. The black mass of flesh crouched suddenly, and, with a grunt, it was in the air, leaping toward the moon before crashing to earth a few yards in front of Zoe and Norman. Dust rose up; several car alarms went off.

Walter grinned, his whiskers twitching in anticipation of violence.

"Almost didn't find you, baby," he growled. "Saw my machine all twisted up on the highway, poked around a little bit, maybe figured you for dead. Sure didn't expect to find you in some hotel with this little cabbage sack."

Norman spent several seconds spitting out random syllables. "Who... Who is that?" he said, finally.

"The walrus," Zoe answered.

His face holes widened in surprise. "Walrus?"

"I'm a god damned pinniped, bitch! Name's Walter, since Zoe don't feel polite enough for introductions. *Odobenus rosmarus*. Four-thousand pounds of 'I'm gonna beat your ass until your dick bleeds.'"

Walter lunged forward, surprisingly fast for such a large animal. Norman fell on his butt and sat like a doll, unsure of how to proceed.

"Walter! Stop it!" cried Zoe, but he shoved her aside with his enormous tail. She hit the dirt with a loud, dusty thump.

"I'm going to knock every one of your tiny human teeth down your throat, hold you upside down by your ankles until you shit them out into your pants, and then I'm going to make you eat your pants!" Walter began to advance with the grace of a semi-truck. He windmilled his flippers.

"Norman, look out! He's crazy!" Though Zoe hated to admit it, the concept of a man and a walrus battling over her made her nipples hard.

"No, I'm not going to cave in to this guy!" Norman picked himself up. "I am a man of infinite resources!"

The walrus just stared for a moment, then scratched himself.

Norman turned to Zoe. "You shared something special with me last night," he told her.

"There's a lot more, Norman," she replied. "Deeply personal stuff. I was trying to tell you when everything went to hell!"

61

Walter's bellow was a bomb. "What have you been up to, you pile of shit?"

Zoe whipped around. "Nothing, Walter! Just go away! I'm making friends!"

Norman laid his hand on her shoulder. "It's my turn to share something with you. I have a secret weapon."

He steeled himself. Zoe and Walter looked on quizzically.

"Okay, boys, it's time," Norman whispered. He began humming upbeat action movie music, imagining how incredibly cool he looked. The eyeless holes in his face rippled and pushed as, one by one, the party wolves emerged from his empty sockets.

Rex, Cooter, Sophie, Smitty and even Herb "The Herb" were wearing their best combat-ready expressions. Steely eyes glinted in the darkness; tongues lolled out of the sides of mouths.

"That's right, you saber-toothed lard bucket," Norman taunted, proudly. "Meet the party wolves. They're my army, and you touch one hair on my ass, they're going to fuck your world up with crazy lobo violence!"

Zoe and Walter both stared at the small army of party wolves that had exited Norman's face.

"Norman, honey," Zoe said. She sounded confused.

"What?" Norman whispered back. "I'm in the middle of a showdown."

"Norman, those aren't... Isn't that your dog?"

Walter threw his gigantic head back and blubbered with laughter.

The party wolves shifted around uncomfortably. Smitty looked like he was about to puke, having ingested a tad too much guarana all at once, so he sat down and started licking his balls to comfort himself. The rest looked embarrassed.

"You're going to sic *those* on me?" Walter snorted.

Norman was indignant. "What? What's wrong with these? Why are you laughing? Because you think this is funny, or because you're nervous, you stupid sea cow?"

The walrus immediately stopped laughing, hatred glowing in his tiny eyes. "Don't call me a fucking manatee, flesh-sack."

"What are you going to do about it, whisker-face? You look like you have pubic hair growing from your nose!"

Zoe's face was a mask of warning. "Norman, stop. You're making him madder."

"What's he going to do? I have my party wolves at my side! Wolves, baby!"

"Norman, sugar, listen," Zoe said. "Those are coyotes."

The only sound came from crickets in the surrounding fields.

Norman's stomach felt sour and knotted. "Party wolves," he said to them. "You said you were party *wolves.*"

"Norman, buddy, be cool," Cooter barked.

"Okay, so maybe we lied about being wolves, per se, but man, don't blow our rep, kay?"

"Being a wolf is a state of mind," yelped Rex, who still looked tough, but was rapidly diminishing in machismo. "You can be anything! This is America, man!"

"Can you excuse us a second?" Norman asked.

Walter nodded, flippers folded across his ample chest.

Norman pulled Cooter aside. The rest of the coyotes followed them. "What the hell? Coyotes? You're pretending to be wolves?"

"Wolves, coyotes, puppies," Herb "The Herb" grinned, then added, "Cousins?"

"Chill out," squeaked Smitty. "Like you've never lied on a resume before."

"I've never told anyone I was a prize fighter instead of a tech support guy!" Norman fumed.

"Is this going to screw up our security deposit situation?" Cooter asked.

"We'll talk about it later. But you can still beat up an overgrown fucking harp seal, can't you? I mean, I know he's got swords on his face, but you have jaws, and jungle knowledge, and tribal wisdom, right?"

Zoe hurried to Norman's side. She grabbed his arm. "Norman, we have to go!"

"No," he said. "We have to teach him not to mess with us, or he's going to keep coming."

"Having your dogs do your work?" Walter taunted. "What kind of man are you?"

Cooter raised the hair on the back of his neck and went into a crouch. "Okay, seriously you guys, he's a sheep," he said, stoically. "Think of him as a sheep."

The rest of the crew followed in suit, and to everyone's surprise, including their own, the coyotes formed a formidable little collection of fur and fangs.

"Finally," Walter said. "I want to kill you in time for lunch." He winked lasciviously at Zoe. "Plus, I want to fuck the shit out of my girlfriend."

"I'm not your girlfriend anymore!" Zoe screamed.

"Yes, you are!" Walter roared.

"To arms, men!" Norman shouted. "Show this asshole what you've got!"

"You want to rumble, you peachy little meat bag?" Walter fished around in a money-belt sandwiched between two folds of gray fat. When his flipper returned from the wrinkle, it held a large cotton swab, the kind used to clean out a baby's ear canal, only this one had swabs the size of a normal human baby's skull.

Zoe dragged Norman toward the vehicle.

The walrus jammed the swab into his ear and started twisting. Mounds of waxy brown gunk plopped out and splattered on a nearby pick-up truck, some of it oozing down the side of the walrus' vast bulk.

Walter hummed a jaunty little tune as he cleaned out his other ear, chunks of reddish brown crust falling like snowflakes. When he was done, he stuck the giant swab in his mouth and began to suck off the goop, loudly. Norman couldn't help himself; he leaned sideways and vomited a thin, watery stream onto the parking lot surface. Walter saw this and laughed.

"What? It's delicious," Walter said with a mean-spirited chuckle, waxy gunk still dripping from his whiskered lips.

"Frosted Christ on a stick, Norman!" Zoe screamed. "You don't get it! We have to go!"

Norman looked up once again, and saw Walter posed like a Norse God in the streaming moonlight, a sinister grin plastered on his fat mouth. A faint howling, like the sound of a tornado, arose from somewhere in front of him.

That's when the walrus's face began to distort like a melting stick of butter.

Chapter Fourteen

Giant black paws emerged from both sides of the walrus's head, followed by muscular forearms and haunches. The paws flexed and claws popped out, grabbing hold of the copious flesh surrounding the shoulders of the beast and pulling at it. A series of large, black wolves burst from inside Walter, each bigger and meaner than the last.

Nearly as long as Norman was tall, the black wolves were covered in fur that looked spiky, like it was dipped in pomade. They stood tall and stiff-legged, ears forward, eyes staring at Norman's little band.

The coyotes immediately dropped into attack positions and tried to make themselves appear as large as possible. Even Rex looked anxious, his tail tucked low, ears flattened.

Walter's voice boomed. "Hey boys, these guys say they're party wolves. Should we show them how to party?"

Rex stepped forward. His eyes shifted back and forth as he waited for one of the larger wolves to make the first move. Smitty did his best to imitate a karate pose, but failed miserably.

Suddenly, one of the giant black beasts leapt across the expanse between the two miniature armies and slammed full-force into Rex. The growling cyclone that ensued rolled backward and knocked Herb "The Herb" aside. Disoriented, he threw up.

Rex rolled over the giant black wolf, maneuvering himself into a position of power, and used his weight and the momentum of his body to fling the wolf to the ground. He then boosted himself atop of the larger beast's back and sunk his fangs deep into the neck of the monster. The wolf howled and tried to throw Rex off, but the tenacious coyote ground his jaws onto the loose skin like a bear-trap. Another of the larger wolves rushed to aid his compatriot and butted Rex to the ground. Rex did a barrel roll, came up snarling, but was outmatched.

"I'm going to die," Norman groaned.

Bellowing, the walrus charged, giant black wolves flanking him on either side. Rex had regained his advantage by slamming himself into both larger wolves at once, knocking them off balance. He clambered back atop his adversary and nipped at the wolf's ears, but the wolf kicked up and sent Rex flying, head-over-heels, into the dust. Immediately, two of the others were upon him, jaws pinning Rex in a vicious imitation of a guillotine.

Meanwhile, Smitty cursed wildly as another wolf sat on him. Herb lay in a pile of his own filth, too sick to move. Cooter attempted to outmaneuver the final wolf, endlessly circling like a shark trying to defeat an ocean liner. Sophie crept around the walrus toward Zoe. Her stealth seemed to work until, as she scrambled the last few feet around the enemy, Walter reared back his head and brought his enormous jaws forward, slicing Sophie's haunch with his tusk. She crumpled to the pavement.

Walter charged at Norman, gleaming flecks of blood shining off his tusks. At the moment of impact, Norman's tender frame buckled. His ribs ached as he flew backward and slammed into the side of a dumpster some fifteen feet away. As he slid down it, he felt a growing warm sensation, one part pain, one part piss in his pants.

The dumpster vibrated as Walter continued his charge. Norman steeled himself for a death-blow. All around him came the sounds of his party wolves, who he had really begun to see as friends—perhaps his only ones. They moaned, whimpered and howled in agony. He prepared to make his last words, "I'm sorry," when he heard Zoe shout over the cacophony.

"Walter! Take a look at these, you slut!"

Everything stopped, suspended in a moment of silence. Norman wished he could see what was going on. Was Zoe showing off her tits?

"Come on, you piece of shit. Are these what you want? You know you do!"

The walrus turned to Zoe, the anger in his face replaced by desire.

"Well, Walter?" she said. "They're ice cold and need a good licking."

Walter chuckled to himself and moved closer to Zoe. She stood in the dim light of the early morning, tall, sensual and proud. She had removed her stilts, ankle and foot wrappings. Instead of feet, she had a pair of three-foot tall Emperor Penguins.

"HONK!"

Zoe put her right leg forward and wiggled the penguin in a coquettish manner, causing Walter to salivate.

"That's right, big guy. Can you smell them? They've been wrapped up for so long they're practically marinated. I know you want a taste."

Walter took off in a mad scramble to reach the moist and clearly uncomfortable penguins. Blinded by lust, he didn't notice Zoe's taser. It lit the walrus up with 50,000 volts.

"Y-y-you fuh-fuh-fuh—whore!" he sputtered as his tail thrashed and knocked most of the wolves and coyotes around him upside down and sideways.

Zoe shot past Walter and grabbed Norman's hand, dragging him toward their car. The black wolves looked back and forth between the departing duo and their pinniped boss; the coyotes gathered themselves up and raced across the lot.

Norman pawed at Zoe's penguin feet, which were cooing softly and flapping their wings.

"Those are amazing," Norman said, poking at the dapper birds. "You were afraid to tell me about them? Really? I have *coyotes* living in my *skull*."

The mass of coyotes, following close behind, were a bloody, hairy clump of sad faces and broken dreams. Without a word, they piled into the car. Zoe revved the engine as an angry roar crashed over them.

"I'll kill you all! No mercy! You're dead!" screamed Walter. The black wolves were trying to help him up, but he was too heavy for them. "Don't worry about me! Stop that car!" he cried.

The giant wolves sprinted on muscular legs, but they weren't fast enough to catch it. Zoe stepped on the gas pedal and tore out of the parking lot, leaving a ranting, raving, car-destroying walrus smashing everything in sight, cursing the very air.

Chapter Fifteen

The hum of the sedan's engine just covered the soft, pained whimpers of the coyotes, who again rested inside Norman's skull. He turned toward Zoe, not sure how he should feel.

"Okay, so there's obviously a lot you aren't telling me. I think it's time we come clean." Norman stared down Zoe. She shrank into the driver's seat. "He had wolves in his head. Big, mean, vicious, snarling wolves. Don't you think that's something you should have mentioned earlier?"

"You had coyotes and didn't say a damned thing." Zoe accelerated slightly. Dawn was on the horizon, sending spider webs of light through a thin layer of stratus clouds.

"What about your penguins?" asked Norman.

"What about them?"

"It all makes sense now. Your constant craving for the cold. The mysterious honking. Your unusual height," Norman started, just before Zoe reached over and punched him in the arm.

"Ow!"

"I've always been tall for my age."

"You have penguins for feet!" Norman cried, then looked down at her penguins. Both stared up at him. One honked. "Shut up!" he shrieked. "This isn't funny!"

"Don't tell them to shut up, Mister den-for-a-face!" Zoe retorted. "They're the reason you're still alive!"

Norman considered this. "Okay, I'm sorry. Let's just agree that both of us were holding some pretty important cards close to our chests. And let me call attention to the one-ton walrus in the room. That's not a metaphor."

Zoe sighed heavily, set the cruise control. "We were supposed to get married."

"You were supposed to marry that?" he sputtered. "How do you even... Where can... I mean, how can a woman marry a four-thousand pound sea mammal."

"Tagus, North Dakota. That's why I recognized the

brochure that your little friends were carrying around." She looked at Norman questioningly. His expression was indecipherable. She continued: "Walter introduced me to the place when he started talking about marriage. Story is that there's a cult there that'll marry anyone to anything. Any religion under three-thousand years old or so doesn't survive long in Tagus. They're interested in things that go back to the very beginning."

"The beginning of what?" Norman asked.

"*Everything*. Walter said they worship the primary components of life itself. Pieces and parts of the whole, shapes and forms."

They sat quietly for a moment, feeling a weighty silence descend on the car. Norman put his hand on Zoe's. She didn't move it away.

"From now on, no more secrets," he said.

Zoe turned her hand over and squeezed Norman's fingers.

"I need to check on the coyotes," he said before turning himself inward.

Rex and Sophie were nowhere to be found, and neither was Smitty. Only Cooter and Herb "The Herb" remained in the frontal lobe of Norman Spooter's skull, and the pair looked very depressed.

"Wolves, wolves, party wolves," whimpered Herb "The Herb" as Cooter stared into Norman's floating, ethereal consciousness. It bathed the inside of his brain in a blue glow.

"Come on, man. Don't drop that coyote vibe on us, 'kay?" Cooter pleaded. "You're rubbing salt in the wound."

"Why didn't you just tell me? You made me look like an idiot back there and almost got us all killed!"

Cooter frowned. "No, man, *you* almost got *us* killed. We were doing you a favor." He sat on his haunches, then slowly brought himself down to the ground and laid his head on his front paws.

Norman noticed the matted fur at the corners of Cooter's eyes. He wondered if coyotes could cry, and decided that they could, and immediately felt awful. "Look, I'm sorry. This hasn't been easy for me to deal with."

"We're good neighbors," Cooter prodded. "We don't pee on anything, or chew on your brainstem."

"I know, but having someone—anyone—living in...well, where my eyes used to... Forget it. Do you have any pills?"

Cooter moved toward a small snuffbox on one of the bookshelves. "First one's on me. Call it a let's-be-friends gift."

"Just take a handful of whatever you've got and jam it into an artery," Norman replied. "We're heading to a place called Tagus. I might need you guys to watch my back one more time."

Cooter nodded. "Okay, dude, we'll keep an eye out." The coyote snickered. "Get it?" Cooter paused a moment, then looked indignant. "You deserve all the bad puns I throw at you. Smitty has a walrus bite. Sophie needed stitches."

"Cooter, come on! I didn't ask for this!"

A low growl came from the darkness of the hallway, next to the tip of Norman's medulla oblongata. "*You* didn't ask for this?" Rex stepped out of the hall. His fur was spotted with drying blood, which he was untangling with a switchblade comb. His pompadour was a mess. His eyes were amber, but flecked with tiny reddish stones that made him look psychotic. "*None* of us asked for this." Rex turned toward Cooter, who backed away, slowly. "Cooter, when we moved in here, you kept saying that everything would be cool, but look at us. When's the party? In between the massive rumbles with walruses? Is my twisted ankle part of the party? Or all these bruises and scrapes on my flank? What about Sophie? If she'd been seriously hurt, I'd be tearing his cerebellum in half. Look at my hair, Cooter. Shit!"

Norman fidgeted nervously. Cooter piped up, "You just have to relax, Rex."

Rex gestured at the inside of Norman's skull. "This guy, he's fucking us left and right. I don't care how cheap the rent is. Sophie and I should have just moved into a regular apartment. Spooter, you're a mess, and we live in *your* head? I should eat your central nervous system right now, save us all the trouble!"

"Look, I'm sorry—" Norman stammered.

"Sorry won't cut it! What's to keep us from just handing you over to the walrus? What do we care about you and that chick?"

Simultaneously, everyone realized this was indeed the question. An uncomfortable silence fell.

"This guy didn't make fun," said a small, squeaky voice from the corner. Smitty came out, a crutch underneath his haunch. "He didn't make fun of my height, or your James Dean rip-off style, or Herb's dead-eyed stoner gaze." A proud edge entered Smitty's voice. "Most important of all, he knows we're just coyotes now, and he's not calling us puppies. He's not making howling-at-the-moon jokes;

he's not calling us scavengers. He's asking for our help, Rex. When's the last time someone actually thought we were worth taking seriously? Even our own pack called us slackers, poseurs; we were outcasts. But this guy? He's all right with me."

Smitty, aching from being sat on by a few hundred pounds of wolves, hobbled to the front of Norman's skull and rested a paw on the frontal lobe. Norman felt a sense of warmth creep through his head. "Sometimes you gotta give people the benefit of the doubt," the little party wolf said.

Rex's jaw hung down in amazement. He watched as Herb emerged, a gigantic joint in his paw, and crossed the brainpan to join Cooter and Smitty. Looking around, he saw Sophie standing just behind him.

"Baby? You don't buy this, do you?" he whined, eyes pleading.

Sophie held out her silky, furred arms to Rex and placed her paws on his. "Rex, honey, we're all in this together."

Rex would never admit it, but she was right. He needed a pack. Even tough guys had gangs to watch their backs. Norman had also bought them snacks. His stomach rumbled.

"You going to buy us more jerky, you big, hairless monkey?" he asked, growling.

Norman projected his response. "Rex, if we survive this, I'll buy you a whole cow."

Rex nodded and flipped up the collar on his leather jacket. He licked Sophie behind the ears, and the tension dissipated.

"Norman?" Zoe asked, snapping her fingers in front of his face.

He shook himself out of it and rubbed his temples. "Sorry, I wasn't listening," he said. "What were we talking about?"

"I was telling you that I was about to marry a walrus."

"Can I ask why?"

"Well, I joined this club. Neat people—did fun things together, you know?"

"Like a youth group?"

"Kind of. Basically a singles club for walrus-human bonding." She hoped that his face would flash with either recognition or sympathy. Getting neither, she continued. "Cult of the Buttered Walrus."

"I'm going to stop you right there," Norman said. "I saw the *60 Minutes* special."

"Propaganda!" Zoe screamed, then looked embarrassed. "Sorry, the indoctrination kind of sticks with you."

71

Overhead, the sky darkened, and the closer to Tagus they got, the more clouds rolled in, until finally, the only illumination was from their headlights. North Dakota had a population of about twelve people, and, apparently, all were in bed. Zoe and Norman shuddered as they rolled on through the night.

Chapter Sixteen

In Tagus, a couple of old-fashioned streetlamps cast a dull, aching glow over the dusty roads, now blank and soulless. An old sign above a window bespoke the presence of a bar, and little else. Long-abandoned houses stood like empty graves, their windows making faces at the night, doors laughing as wind blew over the old boards. The sky itself was a midnight blue, the black silhouette of a steeple standing out against it like a coal deposit, stabbing the gloom.

Norman and Zoe walked with vigilance through the streets. The coyotes had explained to Norman that they were great in the dark, that they would keep an eye out from the periphery like snipers. Presumably, they were nearby, prowling the outskirts.

"See anything?" Norman asked.

"Nope," said Zoe. "Just lots of rubble. Let's hurry up and find your eyeballs so we can get out of here."

A noise suddenly shattered the silence, making both humans jump. Smitty crouched in the darkness, howling up at the moon. He stopped short when he realized that Norman, Zoe and his fellow coyotes were frantically shushing him.

"Sorry, man. I can't help it," Smitty whispered. "I'm nervous."

"Too much noise," Rex growled from the shadows. Suddenly, a long, melodious cry curled up from behind him. Sophie howled up at the moon as well, harmonizing with Smitty.

Cooter emerged from the blackness to the left of Rex. "Sorry, Norman. Instincts." Within moments, all the party wolves caterwauled as a chorus. The sound echoed off trees and bounced around town, filling it with night noises.

"Well," said Zoe. "If they didn't know we were here before, they might have a pretty good idea now." Something crunched under Norman's foot. A tiny plastic bottle lay on its side in the gutter. Eyedrops. His eyes had been here, and from the still-moist tip, not long ago.

Zoe grabbed Norman's arm. "Do you hear that? It sounds like an air horn."

The noise originated from somewhere past the trees at the edge of the tiny city park. Two moons blazed through the branches, and the unmistakable sound of hydraulics hissed like cobras ready to bite. The circles of light enlarged as the roar built to a crescendo, and a semi-truck came crashing through the trees.

Walter's grin gleamed by the dashboard light as he barreled down on the group. The coyotes scattered, using their superior speed to scamper out of the path of the oncoming engine. Norman braced himself to feel the brain-rattling death stroke from the grill of Walter's truck. Instead, soft paws slammed into him, sending him sprawling.

Rex drooled and gritted his teeth atop Norman's chest. His breath smelled like raw venison. Grill marks were scraped across his leg, and his paw was bent at an odd angle.

"You saved me," Norman said.

"I guess I did," growled Rex. It was obvious he was in a lot of pain.

Carefully, Norman pulled himself from underneath the injured coyote and stood on shaky legs. "Thanks, Rex."

Rex wagged his tail ever so slightly before clearing his throat with a growl.

Walter had abandoned his stolen truck and was engaged in flipper-to-paw combat with the pack of party wolves. Handily, he took on Sophie, Cooter, Smitty and Herb all at once, laughing as he towered over them. They jumped in and attacked from behind, biting and then moving away before the walrus could will his massive frame to retaliate.

But Walter was no ordinary walrus. Tiny Smitty leapt forward for a nip, but was snatched midair and swung around to block an attack by Cooter. The two coyotes slammed into each other, clumps of fur flying. Sophie clamped down on Walter's back. The walrus roared, then grinned and purposely fell backward on top of her. Sophie yelped in pain, lost completely under layers of blubber.

Herb "The Herb" stared down Walter. The coyote stood on his two rear legs, like a human, and from a pouch around his neck, he pulled a joint and a lighter. He lit up and took a long drag, finally exhaling in the general direction of the walrus.

"Let's do this," said Herb, then he struck a karate pose and screamed, "HIAH!" He brought his arms inward, did

74

a masterful spin kick and landed, paws moving in circles, ready to strike.

Walter threw a car at him.

Herb crashed into the side of a garage, having been totally decimated by a 1973 Gremlin. Walter chuckled and looked around, waiting for his next opponent. Norman called out to Zoe, but received no reply.

Chapter Seventeen

The coyotes were scattered and broken. Zoe was missing. When Norman tried to peer through Hazel and Azul, he saw nothing but blackness no matter how hard he concentrated. Only Norman and Walter, both dirty and bruised, remained.

"Get up," Walter chuckled, lifting Norman by his neck with one huge flipper.

"You don't...have...opposable thumbs..." Norman managed to squeak.

"Taught myself to fold the membranes," Walter said. "*People.* You think you're safe at the top of the food chain, because of your microwaves and speedboats and hair replacement treatments, but you have no idea what I'm capable of!"

The walrus flung Norman upside-down into a pile of metal garbage cans. A series of scrapes and clangs became a symphony in his ears, drowning out Walter's laughter as Norman slid down the edge of a wall and landed with his back bent over one of the cans. Something leaked into his pants. It felt and smelled like coffee grounds mixed with cat urine. He tried to pull himself to his feet, but Walter was already mid-leap.

Walter's vast bulk slammed down on Norman's upper body. Norman coughed, choked and struggled as the walrus ground his enormous ass into his face and farted.

"I can't breathe!" Norman gagged.

"This ain't nothing, stick boy! When I'm done, your lungs will be stretched behind your spine and pulled over your head!"

The walrus reached around and, with a flick of his flipper, flung Norman out from under himself. Norman skidded through the garbage.

"You interrupted my life, meat," Walter continued. "You took my contentment and flushed it." He reared back, wound up and whirled around, hammering his tail into Norman.

The man flew across the street, bouncing off a mailbox. His exhausted muscles could barely move. Sharp pains radiated through them.

At that moment, he regretted that he hadn't been able to help Zoe, or even say goodbye. He was going to die alone, impaled on a tusk, beaten and humiliated by this arctic behemoth. He hadn't even gotten his eyeballs back, and his first renters were lying around like discarded cadavers. It was all very depressing.

Suddenly, the clang of an enormous bell sent shockwaves echoing across the town of Tagus.

"What's happening?" cried Norman.

A cheer went up from somewhere nearby, as did the sound of chanting, a chorus of forgotten languages and cryptic melodies. Rows and rows of human shapes came marching around the corner of the old general store, their faces enshrouded by the overhanging folds of their robes. Norman and Walter paused their conflict in light of this new threat.

Norman tried to listen beyond the noise of the crowd, hoping his friends were seeing this. Weakly, Norman placed his finger into his eyehole and wiggled it around. It was a nauseating and uncomfortable feeling, finger-banging his own face, but the main point was made: no party wolves were in Norman Spooter's skull.

Numerous torches exploded to life amidst the rabble, as one cloaked individual thrust his hands proudly into the air. In these hands, Hazel and Azul lay like royalty, glistening with moisture in the torch-light and looking as smug as two lidless eyeballs could. The bell ceased its mad tolling, and the edge of the mob halted just before overrunning Walter. The walrus backed up and slid against the wall next to Norman.

A large dollop of sweat drizzled off the walrus's husky frame and splashed against Norman's forehead. It smelled like rotting salmon.

Thunder rumbled across the sky; a light rain began to fall. A cultist in a periwinkle robe stepped forward, made some oddly specific gestures in the air and tilted his head toward both man and walrus, waiting for some manner of reply. When none came, he pushed back his hood. The sparse, flickering light revealed his face: that of a fairly nondescript, corn-fed farm boy. What was remarkable, however, was the pair of glasses perched on his nose. They were thick as pancakes.

The leader adjusted his glasses and looked down at

the fighters. When he snapped his fingers, dozens of robed people behind him removed their hoods. All wore thick glasses carved with sigils. The leader yanked on a small silver chain around his neck and pulled a second pair of glasses out of his robe, which he affixed over the glasses on his face. Once those were situated, he reached into a large pocket and removed an old-fashioned spyglass, through which he peered at Norman.

"Good evening. Are you celebrants, or detractors?"

Walter was silent. Norman leaned forward to answer and whacked his forehead on the lens of the spyglass.

"Celebrants, or detractors?" asked the man again.

"Celebrants or detractors..." chanted the crowd.

"My eyeballs," Norman said, arising.

Slowly, Walter lurched his great bulk away from the group, but several of the robed folks noticed this and circled around to block his escape.

"I want them back," Norman continued. "They're mine."

The leader spoke to the eyeballs, holding them high above the crowd. "Do you hear, little ones? This man claims ownership. How do you respond?"

The eyeballs regarded Norman. Instantly, he had the sensation he'd felt before, of looking at himself.

"He is a dictator, a fraud and a jackass," said Azul.

"He smells of hobo ass and smoked garbage," added Hazel, with enthusiasm.

Norman hobbled forward. "I grew those inside my head. I raised them from cells, and they belong to me!" Unused to asserting himself, he felt a tingle in the pit of his stomach.

"What say you, balls of the vision quest? Spheres of the all-seeing? Questers of optic knowledge and squishy-textured lubricated orbs of virtue?" asked the leader. "You came to us for the culmination of your dream of union, and this we have done. Brothers and Sisters, dare we let this interloper tear asunder what we have wrought?"

"Nooooooo!" the crowd thundered in unison.

"To the chamber of spheres!" cried the leader.

The crowd surged forward. Norman felt a dozen hands on his arms and legs, pulling him off his feet. He flailed in their grasp, but it was like fighting against a current. Walter threw cultists in every direction, but the numbers quickly overcame him, and with a dull roar of rage, he disappeared underneath a swell of robed bodies.

Chapter Eighteen

Norman Spooter awoke to the sound of chanting. His arms wouldn't move, nor would his upper body, and he realized that he was tied to a stone slab surrounded by cultists. Every one of them wore novelty glasses, tinted so eyes were invisible. The rain had whipped up fiercely; everything was soaked.

In front of him were the church and steeple. Two simplistically drawn eyeballs were carved above the main doors. Twin circles of approximately twenty feet across—with a tiny solid circle in the middle of each—looked like a pair of giant cartoon tits, with only the fanged mouth of a doorway beneath marking them as facial features. The walls all seemed to meet each other at angles greater than ninety degrees, giving the architecture of the place a weird non-Euclidean geometry.

"It is time!" the leader howled. As the congregation disrobed, Norman found himself staring through Hazel and Azul at nubile young women with enormous breasts. His face grew hot as rain shimmied down their bodies. Walter was in a similar predicament, only they had tied the monster down with steel chains. The expression he wore was one of stifled yet murderous rage.

"Let the ritual begin!" called the leader.

To Norman's surprise, the nude women surrounded his supine body. They began to chant and slink around the altar, eyes rolling back in their heads. *This isn't so bad*, thought Norman.

Simultaneously, as if cued by an unseen stagehand, the women reached underneath the elevated slab and came up holding sinister-looking pairs of needle-nose pliers. They brought their arms down and closed in on Norman's face.

"Oh hell," he said.

"Let the one who denied his eyes freedom be bereft of all imprisoned senses! Tear off his nose! Remove his tongue!

Pull the tiny bones from his ears! We will free them all from this miserable shell!'" shouted the leader.

Norman wanted to cry, but he knew his tears would just fill up his cavities and make his brain soggy. He wished the wolves were here. He wished Zoe was here. Hell, he even wished Walter would somehow free himself, if for no other reason than to provide a needed distraction.

The chanting stopped. Norman breathed in the silence, waiting to feel his features torn from his face. The thunder, too, had ceased for the moment. A gentle rain made the only sound.

The leader lifted his eyes skyward and screamed, "Now, sisters! For the spheres!"

Suddenly, Norman heard a cacophony of car horns, revving engines providing a background of noise and chaos. The rapid pops of gunfire boomed in the night air.

The grounds swarmed with cultists, running for cover. They trampled each other in a mad effort to gain entry to the church. Several were impaled on the teeth that bordered the door, their bodies twitching on spikes, glasses askew and cracked. The door into the building had become a choke point, with cultists beating each other, trying desperately to break the log jam.

In their panic, the cultists securing the hostages forgot their duties, and the bit of slack in his bonds was all that Walter needed. With a mighty roar, he broke free of his chains, sending naked humans tumbling like bowling pins. The cult leader, at the entrance of the church, saw this and scrambled over the mountain of bodies, kicking several in the face. "Tasers! Now! The thing is loose!" he screamed, disappearing from sight just as Walter charged the door and shoved the mass of wriggling bodies through the portal.

Those who remained weren't sure where to turn. Of greatest concern was the cause of the commotion: a long line of jet-black cars, windows tinted like tar. The passenger side windows were cracked just enough to allow the barrels of Gatlin guns to poke out. Every few seconds, they spun to life, a hail of bullets mowing down another handful of cultists. The large-breasted women ran across the yard toward the building. Unfortunately, their bouncing ballast slowed them, and they were cut down en masse.

The yard around the altar had become a mass of mangled flesh, bone shards, spurting blood and severed limbs. Giant titanium and reinforced steel church doors slammed shut. Clearly, the cultists had anticipated such an onslaught.

Beyond, the cars lined up, side-by-side. Norman listened

intently. Walter's roars were fainter and the sounds of his church-devastation less earsplitting. Then there was what sounded like a relieved cheer of triumph. He heard a sliding sound as a little wooden panel unhinged in the wall of the church. A megaphone was thrust through it.

"Interlopers," said the voice behind the megaphone, "we have trapped your walrus in a broom closet! And with only a dozen of our number impaled! We will kill our hostage before allowing you to disrupt our ceremony of freedom! Do not test our resolve!"

The row of cars just sat, engines purring.

The voice called out again: "Do not mistake our intent. We are The Cult of the Twin Spheres, dedicated to all pairs of things round and symmetrical. We only wish to be left in peace to revere the Holy Spheres. If you leave now, we will release the walrus into the wild. We have barricaded ourselves inside the great hall. This door is impenetrable."

Eyeballs, breasts... Norman wondered why they hadn't taken his testicles, but then realized that one hung lower than the other. Maybe his asymmetry was too impure for them.

"You have no choice but cooperate. We have the eyeballs; we have the walrus, and we hold all the cards."

There was a long moment where nothing happened. Bullets on one side, bloody torture on the other, Norman was prepared to will himself to die and deprive everyone of the satisfaction.

The megaphone crackled. "So, are you leaving yet? We're going to get on with the ceremony now. Just...go soon. Thank you."

Very slowly, the passenger side window rolled down on the largest, central car—a classic hearse from the 1950's. A toned, feminine arm emerged, holding a small package from which a rag protruded. Dressed for battle, a penguin arose from the window, a bandoleer across its slippery black and white chest.

"Guess we can't get through the door," a familiar voice called out from inside the vehicle. "Whatever will we do now?" The penguin, attached to a sexy female leg, pulled a wooden match from beneath its wing and struck it against the vehicle. The rag burst into flames.

As the penguin threw the bottle into the air, the other leg appeared from the same window. This penguin was dressed in protective football pads. With a grin, Zoe wound back and booted the bottle, launching it through stained glass above the church doors.

Michael Allen Rose

Moments later, the windows glowed orange. Mixed in with the terrified shrieking of humans burning alive was the bellow of a walrus, roaring with pain and rage, and two tiny voices screaming about the means of production and the ruling class.

Zoe hopped out of the car and ran to Norman. Leaning down, she untied him.

"Zoe, how—?"

She threw her arms around him and leaned in, kissing him deeply. All thoughts of pain and fear melted away as her tongue found his. The flames were starting to rise up now, smoke obscuring the moon. The giant metal door with teeth glowed with heat, scorching the nearby ground.

Finally, Zoe pulled back and looked at Norman. "Hi," she said. "Miss me?"

"What the hell was in that package?" he asked.

"Super-lard. I grabbed it out of Walter's car when we had our accident." At that moment, a squeal built up to a huge, meaty pop. "Goodbye, Walter," Zoe sighed.

Norman put his arms around her shoulders, and they watched the night light up and listened as the screams of burning cultists rose like sparks off the fire.

"Ahem," came a serious-sounding voice from behind them. Momentarily, they had forgotten about the line of death-dealing automobiles. Standing a few feet away, holding an automatic the size of an elephant gun, was a man in a pitch black suit that seemed to swallow up light and color from everything around it.

"Who are you?" asked Norman.

"This is Reverend Pork," said Zoe. "He's a member of the local clergy."

Reverend Pork smiled, and the hairs on Norman's neck stood like soldiers.

"Sure and saints preserve us, Miss," said Mister Pork in a weird Irish brogue, "but there's the matter of payment to be discussed."

"I knew there had to be a group of crazy gun-nuts in this place," Zoe whispered to Norman, "so I went looking as soon as the shit started hitting the fan."

Reverend Pork's voice had the smoothness of snake skin. "You did as you said, Miss. I see the Cult of the Twin Spheres lain before us, a sacrifice to our lord, Charlton Heston—may he reign forever. But where's this super-weapon?"

"Oh shit," Zoe continued. "I told a little white lie. They wouldn't have come unless... well, I told them the cult had

82

a new weapon of mass destruction. Next thing I knew, they were armed and on their way."

Norman seemed puzzled. "What are you saying?"

Reverend Pork motioned to his entourage of hearses. "She's saying we wasted a lot of ammo over your sorry ass, lad."

Zoe reached around in her pockets, but found only lint. She turned to Norman with a grimace. "Got any cash?"

"You lied to my whole congregation. Bend my clover if you aren't in for a world of hurt, lassie." Behind Reverend Pork, his staff climbed out of the hearses, barely visible but for the fire's illumination.

"I'm so tired of being threatened with death," Norman said. Zoe put her hand in his, and they stood there.

"You don't really want to kill us, do you?" she asked.

"Lass, you throw a mean Molotov cocktail. I love watching you work," said Reverend Pork. "But you got us in a fighting mood over a lie, and now there's no worthy sacrifice. He aimed his gun. "Our Lord demands holy gunfire." He smiled. "Any last words before you join those eyeball lickers?"

Suddenly, there was movement. Where there'd been a holy gunslinger, now there was nothing. Then, it happened again. Men in black slipped into the darkness, one by one. Stealthily, Zoe nudged Norman in his ribs. A howl broke the stillness. The reverend looked around and realized his men were missing.

Out of the darkness, Norman's pack exploded with fury, Rex leading the charge. Reverend Pork's face went white.

"Party wolves, go!" barked Rex. Then he sunk his teeth into the reverend's throat. The gun fired wildly into the air. Cooter and Herb each clamped onto an arm as Smitty ripped a hunk out of the man's crotch; Sophie strolled up to Norman and Zoe.

"You guys okay?" she asked.

Norman embraced the she-coyote. "I thought they ran you off, or killed you!"

"We went to lick our wounds and ended up having a little talk," said Sophie over the screams of Reverend Pork. "The consensus was, maybe we *are* coyotes, but that doesn't mean we can't define ourselves however we want."

"That was masterful, Sophie," said Norman.

The she-coyote blushed, although with all the fur in the way, it was hard to tell.

Where Reverend Pork once stood, there was only a

bloody stain and some sticky pieces of meat, which the coyotes picked over. Cooter bounded over to Norman and Zoe. Sophie gave him a quick wink before she headed over to gorge herself on the kill.

"Hey guys," Cooter panted.

"Thanks for everything, Cooter. You guys risked your asses for me," said Norman.

"No problem. We're a pack; we stick together."

"We?"

"We had a lot to talk about, and even Rex said it: You two are basically part of our pack. We travel together, hunt together, eat together...party together," said Cooter. "Sure, you're fur-challenged, but we'd like to consider you honorary pack members."

The penguins shuffled nervously, but Zoe stood firm and smiled at Cooter. "That means a lot."

As conversation ended, the three looked around and felt the gloom of Tagus seep into their souls.

Death was all around them. The town was on fire. Walter was dead. People were melting into fat, deep-frying in the super-lard and being eaten in the dark. When Norman tried to hone in on the eyeballs' point of view, the pain nearly knocked him unconscious. He felt their surfaces peel away, viscous fluids bubbling and delicate membranes popping. His eyeballs were gone, victims of their own hubris.

Epilogue

Norman's house was still as he had left it. The void that emerged with the knowledge that he had forever lost his eyes made his future seem bleak. He needed something to fill the abyss.

Surprising even himself, he asked the Party Wolves to stay. A few days after returning home, he realized that he didn't need his eyes that much after all. What he needed was a purpose. Chasing after his eyeballs had made him feel like he had a clear goal in life, that he wasn't just coasting or surviving until the next paycheck.

But now that his quest was through, there was still a void. Most days, he sat playing cards with his friends, the coyotes. They'd bought him a Braille deck in an attempt to cheer him up, although today he was particularly low.

"You in or out, Norman?" Cooter asked. He was dealing five-card draw poker, and there was a mound of jerky on the table.

"Deal me out this round, guys. I'm going to grab a beer." Norman pushed his chair back. "Want anything?"

"Beer, beer, beer," said Herb. The rest of the coyotes nodded in agreement.

"I'll help you with that," said Sophie, padding to the kitchen after Norman on her agile paws. Her walrus wound hadn't been too deep, and she'd healed quickly.

Norman felt her paw at him as he retrieved a six-pack from the fridge.

"What's the matter, Norman?" The she-coyote looked up at him with big, wet canine eyes, like a house pet.

"I'm okay."

"You're thinking about her, aren't you?"

It had been less than a week since Zoe and he had parted ways. The drive back had proven relatively quiet. They'd even stopped at the home of Amos Droop. After getting his address from registration documents in the glove box, they left the sedan in his front yard with a full gas tank and a big ribbon around it. The thank-you note had simply read: "Feeling much better—thanks for the lift!"

Soon after, however, Norman and Zoe had realized the main thing that they had in common was the hero's journey, and neither of them had the energy or courage to take the leap and talk about how they felt.

Finally, when Zoe dropped Norman and the party wolves off at home, he'd uttered the most difficult and awkward goodbye he'd ever suffered through.

Norman still had trouble admitting to Sophie that he missed Zoe. His mouth opened, but only meaningless sounds came out.

"You have to call her, Norman," said Sophie. "It's not too late."

He turned away, started walking. "No, we have totally different lives."

"Rex and I aren't the same coyote, you know, but we make it work." She paused. "At least we try."

"I'm a coward, Sophie."

In the living room, the other coyotes stared at Norman, shaking their heads.

"Dude, come on," said Cooter. "You drove across the Midwest blind. You're not a coward; you're just nervous. Party wolves go for it, anytime there's an opening."

He had no reply.

Then, there was a knock on the door.

"Did you order a pizza again, Herb?" asked Norman. There was no answer from the table, which he could only assume meant *yes*.

Sighing, Norman popped the door open. Immediately, a familiar voice froze him.

"Hi, Norman."

Zoe stood on the porch, her penguin feet unwrapped in all their glory. She carried a suitcase. The penguins each held a fish on a stick.

"Where've you been?" asked Norman. "Your house?"

"Walter's house. But I can't stay; it's all in his name," she said. "So, I was thinking of moving somewhere. With a couple of nice zoos, in case my feet get lonely."

"What if *you* get lonely?" asked Norman.

Energy seemed to buzz between them. "I don't know. I wanted to say bye, I guess, since I don't know what else to do." She took a deep breath. "Thanks for everything. I couldn't have gotten away from Walter without you. You changed my life."

Zoe hugged Norman. His face flushed, and after a few seconds, she pulled away. The penguins shuffled uncomfortably. She looked into his eyeholes, both of them waiting for the other to say something.

"Oh, for fuck's sake! Kiss her, you stupid monkey!" Rex roared from inside.

Norman blushed as Zoe tried to peer around him. "The coyotes stuck around, huh?" she said.

"I hate to say it, but I kind of like them."

"How did you get them to stay?"

The moos of a cow emerged from somewhere in the back of the house.

"I'd rather not talk about it," said Norman, quietly.

"Shut up, dinner!" Rex barked.

At that moment, Norman felt blood speeding through his veins, every heartbeat a thunderclap in his skull.

It was now or never.

He wrapped his arms around Zoe and squeezed her tight, planting his lips firmly against hers. They'd held the kiss for several seconds when a series of "Whoo-hoos!" came from inside.

"I was hoping you'd do that," Zoe said, smiling.

"I love you." Norman felt light-headed. Had he just said that?

"Oh wow," said Zoe.

"Do you want to come in and warm up?"

"I would, but..." She pointed at her penguin feet. Both looked nervous.

Norman considered the empty void in his life. "Coyotes don't eat penguins," he said. "And I have air conditioning."

Their hands found each other, and, for the first time since Norman had lost his eyeballs and Zoe had left her walrus, they felt like they were part of something bigger.

He picked up her suitcase and brought it inside.

She followed him in and closed the door tight behind her.

ABOUT THE AUTHOR

Michael Allen Rose is a writer, performance artist, producer and musician living in Chicago IL with a cat named Dandelion. Originally from the frozen wastes of North Dakota, Michael's plays have been produced in New York, Chicago, Portland, Denver and several other major cities. He is founder and artistic director of RoShamBo Theatre, and releases industrial and experimental music under the pseudonym Flood Damage. His shorter pieces have been published in Kizuna: Fiction for Japan and seen on stage at Chicago's famed Second City where he spent a year studying at the conservatory.

You can visit him at www.gerbilprobe.com to find out more about his noise, www.roshambotheatre.com to find out more about his performance, and of course www.partywolves.com to find out more about the book you're holding right now.

He would like to take this time to thank all the girls he's ever fallen in love with in alphabetical order, starting with... wait... what? We're out of space? Never mind then.

BIZARRO BOOKS

CATALOG   FALL 2011

ERASERHEAD PRESS

Your major resource for the bizarro fiction genre:

WWW.BIZARROCENTRAL.COM

Introduce yourselves to the bizarro fiction genre and all of its authors with the Bizarro Starter Kit series. Each volume features short novels and short stories by ten of the leading bizarro authors, designed to give you a perfect sampling of the genre for only $10.

BB-0X1
"The Bizarro Starter Kit"
(Orange)

Featuring D. Harlan Wilson, Carlton Mellick III, Jeremy Robert Johnson, Kevin L Donihe, Gina Ranalli, Andre Duza, Vincent W. Sakowski, Steve Beard, John Edward Lawson, and Bruce Taylor. **236 pages $10**

BB-0X2
"The Bizarro Starter Kit"
(Blue)

Featuring Ray Fracalossy, Jeremy C. Shipp, Jordan Krall, Mykle Hansen, Andersen Prunty, Eckhard Gerdes, Bradley Sands, Steve Aylett, Christian TeBordo, and Tony Rauch. **244 pages $10**

BB-0X2
"The Bizarro Starter Kit"
(Purple)

Featuring Russell Edson, Athena Villaverde, David Agranoff, Matthew Revert, Andrew Goldfarb, Jeff Burk, Garrett Cook, Kris Saknussemm, Cody Goodfellow, and Cameron Pierce **264 pages $10**

BB-001"**The Kafka Effekt**" **D. Harlan Wilson** — A collection of forty-four irreal short stories loosely written in the vein of Franz Kafka, with more than a pinch of William S. Burroughs sprinkled on top. **211 pages $14**

BB-002 "**Satan Burger**" **Carlton Mellick III** — The cult novel that put Carlton Mellick III on the map ... Six punks get jobs at a fast food restaurant owned by the devil in a city violently overpopulated by surreal alien cultures. **236 pages $14**

BB-003 "**Some Things Are Better Left Unplugged**" **Vincent Sakwoski** — Join The Man and his Nemesis, the obese tabby, for a nightmare roller coaster ride into this postmodern fantasy. **152 pages $10**

BB-004 "**Shall We Gather At the Garden?**" **Kevin L Donihe** — Donihe's Debut novel. Midgets take over the world, The Church of Lionel Richie vs. The Church of the Byrds, plant porn and more! **244 pages $14**

BB-005 "**Razor Wire Pubic Hair**" **Carlton Mellick III** — A genderless humandildo is purchased by a razor dominatrix and brought into her nightmarish world of bizarre sex and mutilation. **176 pages $11**

BB-006 "**Stranger on the Loose**" **D. Harlan Wilson** — The fiction of Wilson's 2nd collection is planted in the soil of normalcy, but what grows out of that soil is a dark, witty, otherworldly jungle... **228 pages $14**

BB-007 "**The Baby Jesus Butt Plug**" **Carlton Mellick III** — Using clones of the Baby Jesus for anal sex will be the hip sex fetish of the future. **92 pages $10**

BB-008 "**Fishyfleshed**" **Carlton Mellick III** — The world of the past is an illogical flatland lacking in dimension and color, a sick-scape of crispy squid people wandering the desert for no apparent reason. **260 pages $14**

BB-009 **"Dead Bitch Army" Andre Duza** — Step into a world filled with racist teenagers, cannibals, 100 warped Uncle Sams, automobiles with razor-sharp teeth, living graffiti, and a pissed-off zombie bitch out for revenge. **344 pages $16**

BB-010 **"The Menstruating Mall" Carlton Mellick III** — "The Breakfast Club meets Chopping Mall as directed by David Lynch." - Brian Keene **212 pages $12**

BB-011 **"Angel Dust Apocalypse" Jeremy Robert Johnson** — Meth-heads, man-made monsters, and murderous Neo-Nazis. "Seriously amazing short stories..." - Chuck Palahniuk, author of Fight Club **184 pages $11**

BB-012 **"Ocean of Lard" Kevin L Donihe / Carlton Mellick III** — A parody of those old Choose Your Own Adventure kid's books about some very odd pirates sailing on a sea made of animal fat. **176 pages $12**

BB-015 **"Foop!" Chris Genoa** — Strange happenings are going on at Dactyl, Inc, the world's first and only time travel tourism company.
"A surreal pie in the face!" - Christopher Moore **300 pages $14**

BB-020 **"Punk Land" Carlton Mellick III** — In the punk version of Heaven, the anarchist utopia is threatened by corporate fascism and only Goblin, Mortician's sperm, and a blue-mohawked female assassin named Shark Girl can stop them. **284 pages $15**

BB-027 **"Siren Promised" Jeremy Robert Johnson & Alan M Clark** — Nominated for the Bram Stoker Award. A potent mix of bad drugs, bad dreams, brutal bad guys, and surreal/incredible art by Alan M. Clark. **190 pages $13**

BB-031 **"Sea of the Patchwork Cats" Carlton Mellick III** — A quiet dreamlike tale set in the ashes of the human race. For Mellick enthusiasts who also adore The Twilight Zone. **112 pages $10**

BB-032 **"Extinction Journals" Jeremy Robert Johnson** — An uncanny voyage across a newly nuclear America where one man must confront the problems associated with loneliness, insane dieties, radiation, love, and an ever-evolving cockroach suit with a mind of its own. **104 pages $10**

BB-037 **"The Haunted Vagina" Carlton Mellick III** — It's difficult to love a woman whose vagina is a gateway to the world of the dead. **132 pages $10**

BB-043 **"War Slut" Carlton Mellick III** — Part "1984," part "Waiting for Godot," and part action horror video game adaptation of John Carpenter's "The Thing." **116 pages $10**

BB-047 **"Sausagey Santa" Carlton Mellick III** — A bizarro Christmas tale featuring Santa as a piratey mutant with a body made of sausages. 124 pages $10

BB-048 **"Misadventures in a Thumbnail Universe" Vincent Sakowski** — Dive deep into the surreal and satirical realms of neo-classical Blender Fiction, filled with television shoes and flesh-filled skies. **120 pages $10**

BB-053 **"Ballad of a Slow Poisoner" Andrew Goldfarb** — Millford Mutterwurst sat down on a Tuesday to take his afternoon tea, and made the unpleasant discovery that his elbows were becoming flatter. **128 pages $10**

BB-055 **"Help! A Bear is Eating Me" Mykle Hansen** — The bizarro, heartwarming, magical tale of poor planning, hubris and severe blood loss... **150 pages $11**

BB-056 **"Piecemeal June" Jordan Krall** — A man falls in love with a living sex doll, but with love comes danger when her creator comes after her with crab-squid assassins. **90 pages $9**

BB-058 "The Overwhelming Urge" Andersen Prunty — A collection of bizarro tales by Andersen Prunty. **150 pages $11**

BB-059 "Adolf in Wonderland" Carlton Mellick III — A dreamlike adventure that takes a young descendant of Adolf Hitler's design and sends him down the rabbit hole into a world of imperfection and disorder. **180 pages $11**

BB-061 "Ultra Fuckers" Carlton Mellick III — Absurdist suburban horror about a couple who enter an upper middle class gated community but can't find their way out. **108 pages $9**

BB-062 "House of Houses" Kevin L. Donihe — An odd man wants to marry his house. Unfortunately, all of the houses in the world collapse at the same time in the Great House Holocaust. Now he must travel to House Heaven to find his departed fiancee. **172 pages $11**

BB-064 "Squid Pulp Blues" Jordan Krall — In these three bizarro-noir novellas, the reader is thrown into a world of murderers, drugs made from squid parts, deformed gun-toting veterans, and a mischievous apocalyptic donkey. **204 pages $12**

BB-065 "Jack and Mr. Grin" Andersen Prunty — "When Mr. Grin calls you can hear a smile in his voice. Not a warm and friendly smile, but the kind that seizes your spine in fear. You don't need to pay your phone bill to hear it. That smile is in every line of Prunty's prose." - Tom Bradley. **208 pages $12**

BB-066 "Cybernetrix" Carlton Mellick III — What would you do if your normal everyday world was slowly mutating into the video game world from Tron? **212 pages $12**

BB-072 "Zerostrata" Andersen Prunty — Hansel Nothing lives in a tree house, suffers from memory loss, has a very eccentric family, and falls in love with a woman who runs naked through the woods every night. **144 pages $11**

BB-073 **"The Egg Man" Carlton Mellick III** — It is a world where humans reproduce like insects. Children are the property of corporations, and having an enormous ten-foot brain implanted into your skull is a grotesque sexual fetish. Mellick's industrial urban dystopia is one of his darkest and grittiest to date. **184 pages $11**

BB-074 **"Shark Hunting in Paradise Garden" Cameron Pierce** — A group of strange humanoid religious fanatics travel back in time to the Garden of Eden to discover it is invested with hundreds of giant flying maneating sharks. **150 pages $10**

BB-075 **"Apeshit" Carlton Mellick III** - Friday the 13th meets Visitor Q. Six hipster teens go to a cabin in the woods inhabited by a deformed killer. An incredibly fucked-up parody of B-horror movies with a bizarro slant. **192 pages $12**

BB-076 **"Fuckers of Everything on the Crazy Shitting Planet of the Vomit At smosphere" Mykle Hansen** - Three bizarro satires. Monster Cocks, Journey to the Center of Agnes Cuddlebottom, and Crazy Shitting Planet. **228 pages $12**

BB-077 **"The Kissing Bug" Daniel Scott Buck** — In the tradition of Roald Dahl, Tim Burton, and Edward Gorey, comes this bizarro anti-war children's story about a bohemian conenose kissing bug who falls in love with a human woman. **116 pages $10**

BB-078 **"MachoPoni" Lotus Rose** — It's My Little Pony... *Bizarro* style! A long time ago Poniworld was split in two. On one side of the Jagged Line is the Pastel Kingdom, a magical land of music, parties, and positivity. On the other side of the Jagged Line is Dark Kingdom inhabited by an army of undead ponies. **148 pages $11**

BB-079 **"The Faggiest Vampire" Carlton Mellick III** — A Roald Dahl-esque children's story about two faggy vampires who partake in a mustache competition to find out which one is truly the faggiest. **104 pages $10**

BB-080 **"Sky Tongues" Gina Ranalli** — The autobiography of Sky Tongues, the biracial hermaphrodite actress with tongues for fingers. Follow her strange life story as she rises from freak to fame. **204 pages $12**

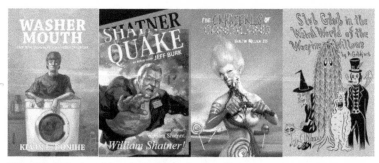

BB-081 **"Washer Mouth" Kevin L. Donihe** - A washing machine becomes human and pursues his dream of meeting his favorite soap opera star. **244 pages $11**

BB-082 **"Shatnerquake" Jeff Burk** - All of the characters ever played by William Shatner are suddenly sucked into our world. Their mission: hunt down and destroy the real William Shatner. **100 pages $10**

BB-083 **"The Cannibals of Candyland" Carlton Mellick III** - There exists a race of cannibals that are made of candy. They live in an underground world made out of candy. One man has dedicated his life to killing them all. **170 pages $11**

BB-084 **"Slub Glub in the Weird World of the Weeping Willows"**
Andrew Goldfarb - The charming tale of a blue glob named Slub Glub who helps the weeping willows whose tears are flooding the earth. There are also hyenas, ghosts, and a voodoo priest **100 pages $10**

BB-085 **"Super Fetus" Adam Pepper** - Try to abort this fetus and he'll kick your ass! **104 pages $10**

BB-086 **"Fistful of Feet" Jordan Krall** - A bizarro tribute to spaghetti westerns, featuring Cthulhu-worshipping Indians, a woman with four feet, a crazed gunman who is obsessed with sucking on candy, Syphilis-ridden mutants, sexually transmitted tattoos, and a house devoted to the freakiest fetishes. **228 pages $12**

BB-087 **"Ass Goblins of Auschwitz" Cameron Pierce** - It's Monty Python meets Nazi exploitation in a surreal nightmare as can only be imagined by Bizarro author Cameron Pierce. **104 pages $10**

BB-088 **"Silent Weapons for Quiet Wars" Cody Goodfellow** - "This is high-end psychological surrealist horror meets bottom-feeding low-life crime in a techno-thrilling science fiction world full of Lovecraft and magic..." -John Skipp **212 pages $12**

BB-089 **"Warrior Wolf Women of the Wasteland" Carlton Mellick III**
— Road Warrior Werewolves versus McDonaldland Mutants...post-apocalyptic fiction has never been quite like this. **316 pages $13**

BB-091 **"Super Giant Monster Time" Jeff Burk** — A tribute to choose your own adventures and Godzilla movies. Will you escape the giant monsters that are rampaging the fuck out of your city and shit? Or will you join the mob of alien-controlled punk rockers causing chaos in the streets? What happens next depends on you. **188 pages $12**

BB-092 **"Perfect Union" Cody Goodfellow** — "Cronenberg's THE FLY on a grand scale: human/insect gene-spliced body horror, where the human hive politics are as shocking as the gore." -John Skipp. **272 pages $13**

BB-093 **"Sunset with a Beard" Carlton Mellick III** — 14 stories of surreal science fiction. **200 pages $12**

BB-094 **"My Fake War" Andersen Prunty** — The absurd tale of an unlikely soldier forced to fight a war that, quite possibly, does not exist. It's Rambo meets Waiting for Godot in this subversive satire of American values and the scope of the human imagination. **128 pages $11**

BB-095 **"Lost in Cat Brain Land" Cameron Pierce** — Sad stories from a surreal world. A fascist mustache, the ghost of Franz Kafka, a desert inside a dead cat. Primordial entities mourn the death of their child. The desperate serve tea to mysterious creatures. A hopeless romantic falls in love with a pterodactyl. And much more. **152 pages $11**

BB-096 **"The Kobold Wizard's Dildo of Enlightenment +2" Carlton Mellick III** — A Dungeons and Dragons parody about a group of people who learn they are only made up characters in an AD&D campaign and must find a way to resist their nerdy teenaged players and retarded dungeon master in order to survive. **232 pages $12**

BB-098 **"A Hundred Horrible Sorrows of Ogner Stump" Andrew Goldfarb** — Goldfarb's acclaimed comic series. A magical and weird journey into the horrors of everyday life. **164 pages $11**

BB-099 "Pickled Apocalypse of Pancake Island" Cameron Pierce—A demented fairy tale about a pickle, a pancake, and the apocalypse. **102 pages $8**

BB-100 "Slag Attack" Andersen Prunty— Slag Attack features four visceral, noir stories about the living, crawling apocalypse. A slag is what survivors are calling the slug-like maggots raining from the sky, burrowing inside people, and hollowing out their flesh and their sanity. **148 pages $11**

BB-101 "Slaughterhouse High" Robert Devereaux—A place where schools are built with secret passageways, rebellious teens get zippers installed in their mouths and genitals, and once a year, on that special night, one couple is slaughtered and the bits of their bodies are kept as souvenirs. **304 pages $13**

BB-102 "The Emerald Burrito of Oz" John Skipp & Marc Levinthal —OZ IS REAL! Magic is real! The gate is really in Kansas! And America is finally allowing Earth tourists to visit this weird-ass, mysterious land. But when Gene of Los Angeles heads off for summer vacation in the Emerald City, little does he know that a war is brewing...a war that could destroy both worlds. **280 pages $13**

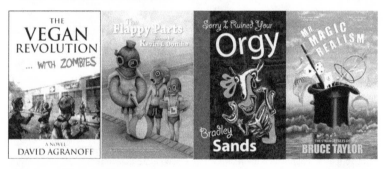

BB-103 "The Vegan Revolution... with Zombies" David Agranoff — When there's no more meat in hell, the vegans will walk the earth. **160 pages $11**

BB-104 "The Flappy Parts" Kevin L Donihe—Poems about bunnies, LSD, and police abuse. You know, things that matter. 132 **pages $11**

BB-105 "Sorry I Ruined Your Orgy" Bradley Sands—Bizarro humorist Bradley Sands returns with one of the strangest, most hilarious collections of the year. **130 pages $11**

BB-106 "Mr. Magic Realism" Bruce Taylor—Like Golden Age science fiction comics written by Freud, *Mr. Magic Realism* is a strange, insightful adventure that spans the furthest reaches of the galaxy, exploring the hidden caverns in the hearts and minds of men, women, aliens, and biomechanical cats. **152 pages $11**

BB-107 "Zombies and Shit" Carlton Mellick III—"Battle Royale" meets "Return of the Living Dead." Mellick's bizarro tribute to the zombie genre. **308 pages $13**

BB-108 "The Cannibal's Guide to Ethical Living" Mykle Hansen—Over a five star French meal of fine wine, organic vegetables and human flesh, a lunatic delivers a witty, chilling, disturbingly sane argument in favor of eating the rich.. **184 pages $11**

BB-109 "Starfish Girl" Athena Villaverde—In a post-apocalyptic underwater dome society, a girl with a starfish growing from her head and an assassin with sea anenome hair are on the run from a gang of mutant fish men. **160 pages $11**

BB-110 "Lick Your Neighbor" Chris Genoa—Mutant ninjas, a talking whale, kung fu masters, maniacal pilgrims, and an alcoholic clown populate Chris Genoa's surreal, darkly comical and unnerving reimagining of the first Thanksgiving. **303 pages $13**

BB-111 "Night of the Assholes" Kevin L. Donihe—A plague of assholes is infecting the countryside. Normal everyday people are transforming into jerks, snobs, dicks, and douchebags. And they all have only one purpose: to make your life a living hell.. **192 pages $11**

BB-112 "Jimmy Plush, Teddy Bear Detective" Garrett Cook—Hardboiled cases of a private detective trapped within a teddy bear body. **180 pages $11**

BB-113 "The Deadheart Shelters" Forrest Armstrong—The hip hop lovechild of William Burroughs and Dali... **144 pages $11**

BB-114 "Eyeballs Growing All Over Me... Again" Tony Raugh—Absurd, surreal, playful, dream-like, whimsical, and a lot of fun to read. **144 pages $11**

BB-115 **"Whargoul" Dave Brockie** — From the killing grounds of Stalingrad to the death camps of the holocaust. From torture chambers in Iraq to race riots in the United States, the Whargoul was there, killing and raping. **244 pages $12**

BB-116 **"By the Time We Leave Here, We'll Be Friends" J. David Osborne** — A David Lynchian nightmare set in a Russian gulag, where its prisoners, guards, traitors, soldiers, lovers, and demons fight for survival and their own rapidly deteriorating humanity. **168 pages $11**

BB-117 **"Christmas on Crack" edited by Carlton Mellick III** — Perverted Christmas Tales for the whole family! . . . as long as every member of your family is over the age of 18. **168 pages $11**

BB-118 **"Crab Town" Carlton Mellick III** — Radiation fetishists, balloon people, mutant crabs, sail-bike road warriors, and a love affair between a woman and an H-Bomb. This is one mean asshole of a city. Welcome to Crab Town. **100 pages $8**

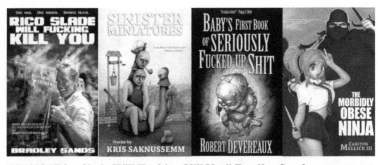

BB-119 **"Rico Slade Will Fucking Kill You" Bradley Sands** — Rico Slade is an action hero. Rico Slade can rip out a throat with his bare hands. Rico Slade's favorite food is the honey-roasted peanut. Rico Slade will fucking kill everyone. A novel. **122 pages $8**

BB-120 **"Sinister Miniatures" Kris Saknussemm** — The definitive collection of short fiction by Kris Saknussemm, confirming that he is one of the best, most daring writers of the weird to emerge in the twenty-first century. **180 pages $11**

BB-121 **"Baby's First Book of Seriously Fucked up Shit" Robert Devereaux** — Ten stories of the strange, the gross, and the just plain fucked up from one of the most original voices in horror. **176 pages $11**

BB-122 **"The Morbidly Obese Ninja" Carlton Mellick III** — These days, if you want to run a successful company . . . you're going to need a lot of ninjas. **92 pages $8**

BB-107 **"Zombies and Shit" Carlton Mellick III**—"Battle Royale" meets "Return of the Living Dead." Mellick's bizarro tribute to the zombie genre. **308 pages $13**

BB-108 **"The Cannibal's Guide to Ethical Living" Mykle Hansen**— Over a five star French meal of fine wine, organic vegetables and human flesh, a lunatic delivers a witty, chilling, disturbingly sane argument in favor of eating the rich.. **184 pages $11**

BB-109 **"Starfish Girl" Athena Villaverde**—In a post-apocalyptic underwater dome society, a girl with a starfish growing from her head and an assassin with sea anenome hair are on the run from a gang of mutant fish men. **160 pages $11**

BB-110 **"Lick Your Neighbor" Chris Genoa**—Mutant ninjas, a talking whale, kung fu masters, maniacal pilgrims, and an alcoholic clown populate Chris Genoa's surreal, darkly comical and unnerving reimagining of the first Thanksgiving. **303 pages $13**

BB-111 **"Night of the Assholes" Kevin L. Donihe**—A plague of assholes is infecting the countryside. Normal everyday people are transforming into jerks, snobs, dicks, and douchebags. And they all have only one purpose: to make your life a living hell.. **192 pages $11**

BB-112 **"Jimmy Plush, Teddy Bear Detective" Garrett Cook**—Hardboiled cases of a private detective trapped within a teddy bear body. **180 pages $11**

BB-113 **"The Deadheart Shelters" Forrest Armstrong**—The hip hop lovechild of William Burroughs and Dali... **144 pages $11**

BB-114 **"Eyeballs Growing All Over Me... Again" Tony Raugh**— Absurd, surreal, playful, dream-like, whimsical, and a lot of fun to read. **144 pages $11**

BB-115 **"Whargoul" Dave Brockie** — From the killing grounds of Stalingrad to the death camps of the holocaust. From torture chambers in Iraq to race riots in the United States, the Whargoul was there, killing and raping. **244 pages $12**

BB-116 **"By the Time We Leave Here, We'll Be Friends" J. David Osborne** — A David Lynchian nightmare set in a Russian gulag, where its prisoners, guards, traitors, soldiers, lovers, and demons fight for survival and their own rapidly deteriorating humanity. **168 pages $11**

BB-117 **"Christmas on Crack" edited by Carlton Mellick III** — Perverted Christmas Tales for the whole family! . . . as long as every member of your family is over the age of 18. **168 pages $11**

BB-118 **"Crab Town" Carlton Mellick III** — Radiation fetishists, balloon people, mutant crabs, sail-bike road warriors, and a love affair between a woman and an H-Bomb. This is one mean asshole of a city. Welcome to Crab Town. **100 pages $8**

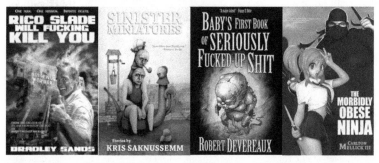

BB-119 **"Rico Slade Will Fucking Kill You" Bradley Sands** — Rico Slade is an action hero. Rico Slade can rip out a throat with his bare hands. Rico Slade's favorite food is the honey-roasted peanut. Rico Slade will fucking kill everyone. A novel. **122 pages $8**

BB-120 **"Sinister Miniatures" Kris Saknussemm** — The definitive collection of short fiction by Kris Saknussemm, confirming that he is one of the best, most daring writers of the weird to emerge in the twenty-first century. **180 pages $11**

BB-121 **"Baby's First Book of Seriously Fucked up Shit" Robert Devereaux** — Ten stories of the strange, the gross, and the just plain fucked up from one of the most original voices in horror. **176 pages $11**

BB-122 **"The Morbidly Obese Ninja" Carlton Mellick III** — These days, if you want to run a successful company . . . you're going to need a lot of ninjas. **92 pages $8**

BB-123 **"Abortion Arcade" Cameron Pierce** — An intoxicating blend of body horror and midnight movie madness, reminiscent of early David Lynch and the splatterpunks at their most sublime. **172 pages $11**

BB-124 **"Black Hole Blues" Patrick Wensink** — A hilarious double helix of country music and physics. **196 pages $11**

BB-125 **"Barbarian Beast Bitches of the Badlands" Carlton Mellick III** — Three prequels and sequels to *Warrior Wolf Women of the Wasteland*. **284 pages $13**

BB-126 **"The Traveling Dildo Salesman" Kevin L. Donihe** — A nightmare comedy about destiny, faith, and sex toys. Also featuring Donihe's most lurid and infamous short stories: *Milky Agitation, Two-Way Santa, The Helen Mower, Living Room Zombies,* and *Revenge of the Living Masturbation Rag*. **108 pages $8**

BB-127 **"Metamorphosis Blues" Bruce Taylor** — Enter a land of love beasts, intergalactic cowboys, and rock 'n roll. A land where Sears Catalogs are doorways to insanity and men keep mysterious black boxes. Welcome to the monstrous mind of Mr. Magic Realism. **136 pages $11**

BB-128 **"The Driver's Guide to Hitting Pedestrians" Andersen Prunty** — A pocket guide to the twenty-three most painful things in life, written by the most well-adjusted man in the universe. **108 pages $8**

BB-129 **"Island of the Super People" Kevin Shamel** — Four students and their anthropology professor journey to a remote island to study its indigenous population. But this is no ordinary native culture. They're super heroes and villains with flesh costumes and out-landish abilities like self-detonation, musical eyelashes, and microwave hands. **194 pages $11**

BB-130 **"Fantastic Orgy" Carlton Mellick III** — Shark Sex, mutant cats, and strange sexually transmitted diseases. Featuring the stories: *Candy-coated, Ear Cat, Fantastic Orgy, City Hobgoblins,* and *Porno in August*. **136 pages $9**

BB-131 **"Cripple Wolf" Jeff Burk** — Part man. Part wolf. 100% crippled. Also including *Punk Rock Nursing Home, Adrift with Space Badgers, Cook for Your Life, Just Another Day in the Park, Frosty and the Full Monty*, and *House of Cats*. **152 pages $10**

BB-132 **"I Knocked Up Satan's Daughter" Carlton Mellick III** — An adorable, violent, fantastical love story. A romantic comedy for the bizarro fiction reader. **152 pages $10**

BB-133 **"A Town Called Suckhole" David W. Barbee** — Far into the future, in the nuclear bowels of post-apocalyptic Dixie, there is a town. A town of derelict mobile homes, ancient junk, and mutant wildlife. A town of slack jawed rednecks who bask in the splendors of moonshine and mud boggin'. A town dedicated to the bloody and demented legacy of the Old South. A town called Suckhole. **144 pages $10**

BB-134 **"Cthulhu Comes to the Vampire Kingdom" Cameron Pierce** — What you'd get if H. P. Lovecraft wrote a Tim Burton animated film. **148 pages $11**

BB-135 **"I am Genghis Cum" Violet LeVoit** — From the savage Arctic tundra to post-partum mutations to your missing daughter's unmarked grave, join visionary madwoman Violet LeVoit in this non-stop eight-story onslaught of full-tilt Bizarro punk lit thrills. **124 pages $9**

BB-136 **"Haunt" Laura Lee Bahr** — A tripping-balls Los Angeles noir, where a mysterious dame drags you through a time-warping Bizarro hall of mirrors. **316 pages $13**

BB-137 **"Amazing Stories of the Flying Spaghetti Monster" edited by Cameron Pierce** — Like an all-spaghetti evening of Adult Swim, the Flying Spaghetti Monster will show you the many realms of His Noodly Appendage. Learn of those who worship him and the lives he touches in distant, mysterious ways. **228 pages $12**

BB-138 **"Wave of Mutilation" Douglas Lain** — A dream-pop exploration of modern architecture and the American identity, *Wave of Mutilation* is a Zen finger trap for the 21st century. **100 pages $8**

CPSIA information can be obtained
at www.ICGtesting.com
Printed in the USA
LVHW111638200422
716665LV00001B/12